MOUNT SKULLS

The Black Cossacks Series
Book Three

Charles Whiting
writing as
Leo Kessler

SAPERE
BOOKS

Also in the Black Cossacks Series
The Black Cossacks
Sabres of the Reich

MOUNTAIN OF SKULLS

Published by Sapere Books.

24 Trafalgar Road, Ilkley, LS29 8HH

saperebooks.com

ISBN: 978-0-85495-513-8

MOUNTAIN OF SKULLS

'The Cossacks are acknowledged traitors!'

British Foreign Secretary, Ernest Bevin, 1945.

The Black Cossacks had come to the end of the road! They had burned, looted, raped, fought their way across half of Europe from the depths of Russia to the mountains of Northern Italy. Always they had fought for their German master because they had believed the Fritzes would allow them to return to their lost homeland on their beloved River Don. But now in the spring of 1945 with the Germans defeated on every front and reeling back under Allied pressure, they knew they would never return. If they ever did go back to Mother Russia, it would be as traitors, who had fought in battle against their Red masters. Men from whom the Soviet dictator, Stalin, would demand the final price for their treachery — death!

So 15,000 Black Cossacks wandered the no-man's land of Northern Italy in the last weeks of the Second World War. Every man's hand was raised against them yet the Cossacks, Russia's warrior elite, continued their last desperate search for independence and freedom. Under the command of General Alexei Bogdan, their great commander who had escaped from a Soviet concentration camp to lead them on their long journey westwards, they fought off allcomers, trying desperately to find a place to establish a new homeland in peace and freedom. Now trusting only their commander and their own curved silver sabres, they rode north into the remote Alps to carve out that new homeland for themselves. THE BLACK COSSACKS WERE ON THE MARCH AGAIN.

BOOK ONE: *ESCAPE INTO THE MOUNTAINS*

CHAPTER 1

The broadfaced civilian in the shabby green overcoat and black cavalry breeches nudged his companion and with a jerk of his head indicated a gap in the gawping crowd. The other man, his face a hideous pink, obviously the result of some terrible war wound, nodded his understanding. With a guttural '*prego*', he pushed his way through the gaping Italians.

Armed partisans wearing the red scarves of the communist brigade, their undernourished bodies hung with looted weapons, were herding a pathetic group of fascist women across the Piazzale Loreto. The women had been stripped to their petticoats and on the front of their shaven heads the partisans had painted the hammer and sickle in scarlet paint. But it was not the half-naked women which the Milanese crowd had come to see this cool April morning.

They had come to see the pile of corpses heaped on the pavement opposite a bombed-out garage. Photographers clustered around them, while the grinning young communist partisans who had shot the fascists only hours before near Lake Como posed heroically every time a camera was turned in their direction.

Suddenly the great crowd gave a gasp. One of the partisans had tossed a rope over a girder and with an accomplice had heaved a body into view — upside down.

'*Il Duce!*' a few of the spectators cried in awe.

But most of them yelled: 'It's that pig Mussolini!' Abruptly the cry went up on all sides: 'String them up — *the lot of them!*'

The grinning communist partisans, sensing an opportunity for more fun, obeyed with alacrity. One after another the members of the last Fascist Government, who had been shot with Mussolini, had ropes tied round their legs and were hauled up. In seconds a whole row of them was hanging like sides of beef.

A woman was strung up. Her brown hair dangled in neat ringlets, but her skirt fell over her plump upper body to reveal her blue silk underwear. A blushing young partisan hastily unbuckled his belt and tugging up the woman's skirt, lashed it into place so that her lower body was covered.

'His whore — it's his whore Clara Petacci, dressed in fancy silk knickers, while we're in rags!' a shrill woman's voice called.

Abruptly the crowd went wild. They surged forward, carrying the two observers with them. A skinny little man darted forward. Before the surprised partisans could stop him, he launched a tremendous kick at Mussolini's head. There was a hideous crunch. Blood jetted in a scarlet stream from the dead dictator's broken nose.

The crowd bayed with pleasure. Screaming and howling like wild animals, the men and women danced and capered around the hanging bodies, as if at some joyous feast. A man ripped off his shirt. Oblivious to the dancing chanting crowd all around him, he set his shirt alight with the aid of his cigarette lighter. '*Presente il Duce!*' he yelled, his right hand stretched out rigidly in the fascist salute. Next moment he thrust his burning shirt into Mussolini's blood-streaked face. There was a sudden stench of burning flesh.

An hysterical woman broke away from the elderly man trying to restrain her. The crowd parted to let her through when they saw the upraised pistol in her hand. 'Five sons, the pig took from me in this war. *Five!*'

She levelled the pistol at Mussolini's body and pulled the trigger. The slug struck the Duce's naked upper body at close range and set it swinging wildly from side to side. The crowd cheered and yelled 'Five!'

'Yes, five!' she yelled back crazily and fired again.

When she had pumped five shots into the dead man, she flung the pistol away and her body racked with sobs, she disappeared back into the crowd.

But there were others to take her place. A fat, heavy breasted woman positioned herself in front of the dangling bleeding Mussolini and raised her skirts to reveal her beefy white legs. Suddenly she grunted and began to urinate over Mussolini's upturned face.

It was too much even for the partisans. One of their commanders ordered his men to fire into the air to make the crowd move back. But there was no holding the Milanese. They did not seem even to hear the rattle of small arms fire. Hacking, cursing, screaming, their eyes crazy with primeval rage, they began to trample on the corpses. As all the bells of Milan started to peal as a signal that the hated dictatorship had finally come to an end, the mob began to strip Mussolini's breeches off him to carry out the last terrible indignity.

But the big man had seen enough. He whispered something to his companion. Together they pushed their way through the hysterical crowd and walked swiftly to the spot where they had hidden their horses in a narrow passage.

Five minutes later they had skirted the crowd and were riding north again.

'Well, what now, General?' Major Boris, the Black Cossack Division's Chief of Staff, broke the long silence as they cantered down the deserted Italian country road.

The man in the green coat, General Alexei Bogdan, Commander of the Black Cossacks, frowned. Instinctively he touched the leather sack of soil from his native Don, which hung around his neck. When he died that soil would be sprinkled in his grave so that he would be buried in his native earth, as the Cossack custom demanded. 'We cannot surrender to those partisan pigs, Boris, that is for certain,' he said at last. 'They would slaughter the Division in cold blood — and we've got to think of our women too.'

Boris nodded his understanding. That morning they had ridden down from the Division's holding position east of Milan intending to surrender the Black Cossacks to the Italian authorities before the advancing Allies took Milan. The whole German front was breaking up and the Black Cossacks, who had fought for the Germans for the last three years, did not want to surrender to the Anglo-Americans along with the rest of the *Wehrmacht* in Italy. They wanted to preserve their separate identity.

'Do we continue to retreat with the Fritzes, General?' he asked.

'No,' Bogdan snapped, reining in his big white stallion Don, and glaring angrily at his Chief of Staff. 'We're not going down with that particular ship, Boris. They have lied to us and betrayed us for too long for us to make that kind of sacrifice. Remember Warsaw?'

Boris nodded his head sagely.

'What did we get for our loyalty to a lost cause after the last war, Boris? I shall tell you. Nothing! Our lands were taken from us and the Don Cossacks were scattered across the face of the earth like the Jews of old.' The General contained his anger at the injustice which had been done to his people nearly a quarter of a century before. 'No, I will not allow that to happen to my Black Cossacks this time, Boris.'

'But what can we do, General?' Boris protested. 'We can't run with the Germans. We can't surrender to the Italians and our quarrel is with the Soviets alone. So we cannot fight the Anglo-Americans — and I hate to think what might happen to us if we were forced to surrender to them. What is left to us, General?'

Easily Bogdan patted the bent neck of his stallion as it ate the parched, cropped grass. 'Don't worry, Boris, there is a way out. What have Cossacks always done when there seemed no way out of some desperate situation?' He raised his arm and pointed to the gleaming white peaks of the far Alps. 'I shall tell you. They fled into the mountains and dared their enemies to come in and fetch them out.'

'You mean up there?' Boris asked, a light of new hope coming into his eyes.

'Yes, up there, Boris. The Allies won't worry us — they'll be too busy pushing on into Austria and fighting the Fritzes. As for the Partisans, whatever shade of scarf they wear, my Black Cossacks will take care of them.'

'By the Holy Virgin of Kazan,' Boris exclaimed enthusiastically, 'we'll start a new Cossackia up there!'

At a gallop the two Cossacks, inspired by new hope, raced up the road towards the mountains and their date with destiny.

CHAPTER 2

The main roads leading north out of Bolzano into the mountains were jammed. The frightened survivors of the defeated German and Italian Fascist Armies were fleeing before the victorious Allies. Advancing like an army of ants, they plundered every farm, every cottage, every hamlet in their path, seizing anything with wheels to hasten their flight — wood-burning trucks, carriages drawn by lumbering oxen, skinny-ribbed ancient nags.

But there were many without transport. Bits of cloth tied around their feet, their eyes empty of hope, they shuffled forward past the dead bodies of their comrades which lay in the ditches like abandoned bundles of rags.

General Bogdan in charge of the advance squadron of the Black Cossacks raised his hand, and behind him the cavalrymen reined in their mounts. Wearily the General wiped the sweat off his brow and tilted his black fur cap to a more comfortable angle. 'This is no damned good, Boris,' he said.

'We could ride them down, General,' Boris suggested.

'Impossible, Boris. There are just too many of them. We couldn't do it. No, we'll have to attempt to go cross-country.'

Boris whistled between his steel teeth softly. 'That's partisan country, General. I've been expecting them to attack this road for the last half an hour.'

'I know, I know, Boris.' Lifting his binoculars, the General surveyed the countryside to the north.

It was spread out in front of them like a map: farm buildings and groves of trees set out in chess board fashion as the ground rose towards the mountains, their peaks streaked with snow and shining in the April sun. It was ideal ambush country, capable of concealing whole regiments of partisans. It was tough country to travel through. But he had no alternative. He made his decision. 'I'll take the lead with the reconnaissance squadron, Boris,' he announced. 'We'll put out squadrons to left and right, grouping the main body of the Division with civilians in their carts to the centre. That should discourage any of your famed partisans from having a crack at us, I think.'

Boris hesitated. 'And what if they've got artillery, General? We'll stick out like fleas on a mare's back.'

The General swore viciously. 'Partisans don't have artillery, Boris. What are you pissing in your breeches for, man, get on with it. There'll be no guns up there, I promise you.'

But General Alexei Bogdan was in for a revelation.

'Jesus Christ!' the artillery observer of the 10th US Mountain Division hissed and focused his binoculars hastily, 'willya get a load of that?'

Next to him Sergeant Holmes, his radioman, peered through his glasses at the enemy cavalry, ploughing through the feather grass below. Little figures, dressed in the field grey of the German Army, but with black fur hats tilted jauntily on their heads and wearing silver, gem-encrusted sabres, slid into the gleaming circles of calibrated glass. The officer lowered his binoculars. 'I'll tell you who they are. They're those goddam turncoat Russians. All last winter they've been fighting Tito's Slavs. Now the Krauts want to set the lousy bunch of renegades on to our boys.'

Holmes rolled over onto his back behind the cover of the stone wall and squinted up at the artillery observer. 'What we gonna do about it, sir? I mean they're not exactly Krauts are they?'

The artillery observer snorted and reached for the field phone. 'They're wearing Heinie uniform, ain't they, Sergeant? For my dough, they're Krauts. I'm going to call down a fire mission on the bastards.'

'But they've got women and kids with them in the wagons, sir,' Holmes protested.

'Tough titty! Why don't you take it up with the chaplain when we get back to the battalion.'

The howitzer crews, veterans to the man, carried out the executive officer's instructions with easy efficiency, each gun commander bellowing out the orders to his crew. 'HE ... VT fuse — three, nine, four!'

At each gun, the Number Six forced the heavy shell upright with his knee. Next to him Number Five screwed home the variable time fuse.

'Charge Six!' the executive officer ordered.

Numbers Three and Four tossed six bags of powder into the howitzer. Immediately Six, Five, Four and Three lifted the shell onto the loading tray and rammed it home. Number Two slammed shut the breech.

'Base deflection left two eight zero!'

The Number Two swung his wheel round. The howitzer's snout raised itself menacingly into the air as if scenting an unsuspecting prey. Number Two picked up the firing lanyard and faced his gun commander.

Twenty-seven howitzers stood waiting, ready to swamp the still unseen enemy with their deadly fire. The executive officer glanced along their ranks and snapped an order over his telephone.

'*FIRE!*'

The howitzers thundered. Below the feet of the crews, the earth shivered and in a controlled cyclone of noise, the great 100 pound shells screamed into the still air.

'Squadron —'

General Bogdan never finished his order. The stillness was abruptly ripped apart by the great 155mm shells overhead. Implacably, they slammed into the mass of the Division, five hundred metres to the leading squadron's rear.

The barrage caught the wagon train completely off guard. Wagons shattering like matchwood, and bodies lay in the dust, writhing in agony. Horses broke loose from their traces. Stampeding with panic, eyes wild with terror, they crashed through the dead and dying.

Bogdan recoiled at the horror. But as the second salvo hissed above their heads, he knew he must act. '*Sotnik!*' he cried over the roar at the young curly-haired Captain at his side. 'Where are their observers? They must be up there on the mountainside somewhere?'

The Captain, famed throughout the Division for his keen eyesight, scanned the mountainside for the possible hiding place of the men who were directing the fire. Then he spotted it: a quick bright gleam of glass behind a heap of boulders. 'There, General,' he cried urgently, 'at two o'clock!'

'Come on!' Bogdan ordered.

He dug his silver spurs into Don's sweating flanks. Behind Bogdan, the rest of the squadron followed, curved sabres at the ready, heads bent low over the necks of their mounts. The two observers saw them coming. Holmes dropped his radio and raising his tommy gun, fired a wild burst of lead at the riders. One Cossack slumped over the head of his galloping horse. But still the rest came on, crying hoarsely, and brandishing their gleaming sabres above their heads, carried away by the wild excitement of the charge.

They reached the base of the mountain and expertly spread out in twos and threes and began to pick their way through the rocks. Slugs whined off the boulders all around them, as the two desperate observers tried to ward off the inevitable. Another Cossack groaned suddenly and slumped to the ground just in front of Bogdan. He tugged at Don's bit to avoid trampling over the fallen man, but the horse stumbled and the General pitched over the stallion's head. He hit the ground hard, and was swamped by the thick red mist of unconsciousness. When he came to again, it was already too late.

As the firing stopped and two of the Cossacks helped the General to his feet, the young *sotnik* appeared from behind a boulder fifty metres away and waved his sabre above his head in triumph. Groggily the General shook his head and saw that the sword's silver blade was now stained a bright crimson. 'We've dealt with the bastards General,' he cried exuberantly.

Alexei Bogdan shrugged off the assistance of the two young Cossacks. He clambered up the rocks to where the grinning Captain was standing. 'Where are they?' he demanded gruffly, his head still ringing.

'There, General.' The *sotnik* indicated the two figures crumpled on their faces in the bloody dust next to a shattered radio.

'Why are they on their guts like that?' the General asked a little stupidly, the red mist still blurring his vision.

Contemptuously two of the Cossacks put their boots underneath the dead men's bellies and shoved the inert bodies round for the General's inspection.

Bogdan gasped. But not because the two men's throats had been cut from ear to ear and their eyes gouged out by the *sotnik's* sabre. He gasped because he now was able to recognize the dead men's uniform for the first time.

'What is it, General?' the *sotnik* asked, the look of triumph vanishing from his open young face.

'Nothing.' Bogdan shook his head. There was no point in wasting words now. 'Get back to the troops and get them moving again.'

Hastily the men swung themselves back on their sweating mounts and began to ride back the way they had come, leaving Bogdan staring at the two mutilated bodies, overcome by the awful realization that his Cossacks had killed their first Americans.

CHAPTER 3

General Mark Clark, the Commander of the US Fifth Army, was very angry. Didn't he have enough problems, trying to get some sort of headlines for his Army, with Ike making the running in Germany and grabbing all the Stateside news space? Now the Russian jerk was giving him a hard time.

He glared at the Russian liaison officer to his Army, Colonel Serov, and said: 'But Colonel I can assure you that nothing is being done behind your back. Your authorities in Moscow are being kept fully informed of what is happening in Bolzano.'

'Comrade Stalin does not think so,' Serov answered, his narrow, tight-lipped mouth working as if by steel springs. 'We feel you are negotiating with the Germans behind our back.'

'Colonel,' Clark groaned as if he were only containing his notorious temper by sheer will-power, 'that is not true. The Krauts are not coming across with a definite statement of their intention to surrender all their troops in Italy yet — Kesselring, their Commander in Chief, is still doubtful. So,' he shrugged, 'we can't prejudice the negotiations by any premature announcements of what we're doing up there in Bolzano.'

Colonel Serov seemed not to have heard Clark's words. He tugged at the flabby pouch under his right eye. 'We think our American allies are no longer fighting the Germans, General. We think instead they are halted on the North Italian front, doing nothing, while their Soviet comrades are still fighting for their lives in Austria, Czechoslovakia, Germany.'

'That is not true, Colonel,' Clark snapped coldly, wishing he could kick the yellow-bellied son of a bitch of a Russian out of his office. 'The terrain is mighty tough up there in the mountains and the Krauts are retreating faster than we can keep contact with them. But my doughs are still in there pitching, believe you me. We're still hitting the Krauts wherever they stand and make a fight for it.'

Serov was unimpressed. As a calculated insult, he took out a packet of *Volga* cigarettes. He pinched the long cardboard filter flat and sliding the cigarette into the side of his mouth, lit it with an American issue zippo lighter. While Clark fumed, he exhaled a stream of blue smoke straight into the Army Commander's face and said: 'Which units?'

'Which units — *what*, man?'

'Are still fighting the Fascist enemy.'

'Listen Colonel, I've got doughboys, Brazilians, Britishers, Italians, Frenchmen, Canadians, Algerians, you name it, I've got it under my command. Do you think I can know exactly which particular outfit of a multi-national army like that is in contact with the enemy at the moment?'

Servo smoked on insolently.

Clark muttered an obscenity and hit the button of the 'squawk box' in front of him on the big desk. 'Bill, come on in and fill me in on the Tenth Mountain. At the double!'

Brigadier William McMahon, the Assistant Chief of Staff, came in hurriedly, holding a sheaf of signals. 'The Tenth, General?' Clark nodded grimly, not trusting himself to say anything more at that moment.

'Our last sitrep puts them north-east of Bolzano up in the Groedner Valley. The terrain's pretty rugged and being a mountain division they haven't got much transport to speak of so —'

'Are they in contact with the Krauts, Bill?' Clark interrupted him impatiently.

McMahon flipped through the sheaf of signals. 'In a way, sir,' he said. 'According to this signal, they ran a fire mission at zero eleven hundred this morning,' he hesitated.

'Well get on with it, Bill. Was it a Kraut outfit they hit?'

McMahon flashed a quick look at the Russian Colonel. 'Not exactly, sir.'

'What the Sam Hill do you mean — not exactly?' Clark bawled.

'Well, sir. The forward observation team of the artillery battalion in question suddenly went off the air. So the fire mission stopped there and then. An hour later the battalion sent out an NCO patrol to find out what had happened to the team. According to this signal, sir, the patrol found the artillery observation team dead. They'd had their throats slit and their eyes gouged out.'

'Holy Jesus,' Clark exclaimed. '*Eyes gouged out*! But who did it, Bill? Surely the artillery boys didn't fire a mission and hit nobody.'

'Sure, sir, the patrol found evidence they had scored several direct hits. According to the report there was plenty of wreckage about, but whoever they'd hit had taken their dead and wounded with them.'

'Hell, man, they couldn't just have vanished into thin air. Didn't they leave some sort of trace? Weapons, bits of uniform, gear, you know the sort of thing?'

'It says here that just before the 10th's patrol spotted a company of German SS moving cross-country and had to hightail it, they picked up a broken cavalry sabre,' he hesitated a moment, 'a kind of fur hat like the Russians wear, but it was decorated with the Kraut eagle and swastika.'

Colonel Serov stubbed out his cigarette and sat up suddenly. 'What did you say — a fur cap with a German badge? *Sookin sin!*' Serov cursed excitedly his brown eyes gleaming abruptly.

'What is it, Colonel?' Clark asked.

'I know the unit your men fired at this morning. It is that led by a well-known war criminal, wanted for three years by the *Stavka*, our High Command. It is General Alexei Bogdan's Black Cossacks who have been fighting for the Germans since the Caucasus in 1942. We had thought them to be still in Yugoslavia, but obviously their masters, the Germans, think that such traitors, who have nothing to lose will continue to keep fighting against their own people when the time comes.'

Clark hit back an angry curse and told himself the appearance of the Cossack Division to his front gave him an opportunity to get off the hook. He couldn't afford to offend the Russian Colonel — there were too many pinkos in Washington who would see his career come to an abrupt end in some lousy home slot if he did. All the same he wanted the kudos of having a major German Army of half a million men surrender to him. But he couldn't expect Kesselring to keep on talking turkey if the Fifth still engaged in offensive operations against his beaten troops. But the Krauts wouldn't care what happened to a bunch of Cossack cowboys, he reasoned. He could start ops against them without affecting the Bolzano negotiations and at the same time he could get the damned Russian Colonel off his back. His mind made up, he looked hard at the Russian liaison officer. 'Colonel Serov, you feel that my Army is not fighting against the Germans, eh?'

Serov inclined his head very slightly. His mind too was full of his discovery. If he were able to deliver the head of Alexei Bogdan to Stalin, there would be a promotion in it for him —

and time was running out fast if he were to get those general's stars before the war ended.

'To prove to you, Colonel, that the Fighting Fifth is not sitting on its thumbs, marking time till the Krauts surrender, I'm going to take that Cossack Division out —'

'*Out?*' Serov queried quickly, unfamiliar with the phrase.

'Yes, *out*. Colonel. This day the Tenth US Mountain Division will begin to seek out and destroy those Cossack renegades of yours.'

Serov rose hastily to his feet. 'And General Alexei Bogdan?' he asked.

'I shall deliver his head personally to you,' Clark said cheerfully, 'on a silver platter!'

CHAPTER 4

As the blood-red ball of the sun started to slip over the horizon, they came to the river. General Bogdan reined in his horse, its flanks glistening with sweat, its hooves grey with the dust of the long cross-country trek. Behind him the Division came to a slow halt.

'What do you think?' Boris asked, halting his brown mare next to Bogdan's stallion.

For a moment, the General did not answer. He surveyed the River Gaderbach carefully. There was no obvious ford, but the water did not look deep and the current was not excessively fast. His cavalrymen would be able to cross it without difficulty and with a bit of luck his wagon train would be able to do the same. Nevertheless he did not like the look of the opposite bank. It was steep — perhaps two metres in height — with its crest crowned by a thick fringe of willows. For all he knew they might well conceal a whole regiment of partisans. Something made him feel apprehensive.

'Do you feel it too, General?' Boris asked, noting the look on Bogdan's face.

'What do you mean, Boris?'

'You feel it, General, like I do. In your bones. There's somebody over on the other side waiting for us.'

Bogdan nodded his big head slowly. Rules were for fools; luck was on the side of the officer who followed his instincts. 'I agree, Boris. There is somebody over there waiting for us.' He glanced at the leather map case strapped to his knee. Bruneck, as the Germans called it, nine kilometres to the north was a well-known partisan nest, firmly in the hands of the

Garibaldi Brigade, the most bloodthirsty of the Communist partisan units. It would be no use attempting to cross the river by the bridges there. The Division would have to cross here or nowhere. But he was not going to risk his men on that slope opposite.

He looked at Boris. 'All right, Major, order the Division to bed down on this side of the river for the night. We'll cross at dawn.'

'*Bed down here for the night!*' Boris echoed his words incredulously. 'But that's just inviting trouble, General I must protest…' The words died on his lips as Bogdan gave him a broad wink. 'Bed down for the night, General. Of course, sir!' He swung Bogdan a tremendous salute so that whoever might be watching them at that moment would think everything was running to plan, and wheeling his mare round, trotted back to the waiting troops to issue orders.

'*Molto stupido!*' the Jaguar, the bearded commander of the 1st Battalion of the Garibaldi Brigade, muttered, lowering his glasses. 'They play into our hands.'

'Do you really think they are camping there for the night, Comrade Commander?' Lionheart, the Battalion's Political Commissar, asked.

Half-a-Gun, the eighteen year old second in command, who had gained his nickname when he reported to fight during the Naples Rising, armed with an ancient musket minus its butt, grinned at Jaguar and said: 'No, they're just warming their hands before they cross the river! Of course, they're there for the night. And it's all to the good. The comrades,' he indicated the partisans dug in everywhere behind them on the river bank, 'will be able to see them better in the morning light.' He gave Jaguar a cheeky Neapolitan wink. 'We'll make sure they get their passport to Switzerland, won't we Comrade Commander?'

Jaguar nodded in silence. If the renegade bastards attempted to cross the river in daylight, they certainly would receive their passports to Switzerland — sudden death! Lionheart, whose courage failed to match his nickname, was not so sure. 'But there must be a whole division of them out there, comrades,' he protested, 'and we're only a battalion. Besides didn't General Clark broadcast that we shouldn't take precipitate action against the Germans?'

Jaguar looked at him with undisguised contempt. Lionheart was one of the many who had joined the partisans when it was clear the Germans were defeated. He knew nothing of the agonising privations they had suffered. He had been with them for only two months, obviously hoping for a good position in post-war Communist Italy. 'Do you mean we should let them cross the Gaderbach unopposed, Comrade?' Jaguar responded icily.

'No, no, Comrade Commander! Not that at all. But I mean they are regular troops and we are not. Perhaps if we radioed the Americans —'

'Americans!' Half-a-Gun sneered. 'I fart on them!' To give emphasis to his words, he slapped one hand against the bicep of the other arm in a gesture of absolute contempt.

Jaguar was more precise. 'Perhaps I should recall Comrade Togliatti's words to you, Comrade,' he snapped. 'Our leader has stated publicly, "Don't obey General Mark Clark. It is in our vital interests that the population should destroy the Nazi-Fascists before the Allies arrive. Choose your own moment for insurrection." I am doing exactly that.'

'Of course, of course, Comrade Commander,' Lionheart agreed swiftly, 'I was only thinking of our comrades. Their valuable lives must be saved for the tremendous tasks that await us of the CP in the post-war world —'

Jaguar held up his hand for peace. 'All right, no speeches, Comrade. So you are concerned with the valuable lives of our comrades, eh? Good, then this night you can do something to ensure that nothing happens to them.'

'Anything, Comrade Commander.'

'It appears that those renegades over there have settled down for the night. But we can't be so sure. I want you to take out a patrol as far as Brunico to ensure that they are not making any attempt to cross the river higher up.' Jaguar raised his clenched right fist and snapped the Garibaldi Brigade's motto, 'No passes, no golden bridges for those retreating — only a war of extermination!'

Lionheart echoed the words without conviction and remained crouching fearfully in the bushes.

Jaguar cleared his throat angrily. 'Well, man, you have your orders, get on with it!'

'*Sì, sì, subito!*' Reluctantly the Political Commissar doubled across to the men crouching in their foxholes to pick his patrol.

Five minutes later when the partisan patrol, heavily laden with weapons and belts of machine gun ammunition, started to move out in single file, Jaguar rose to his feet and said, '*in bocca al lupo.*'

'*Grazie!*' the young man replied.

Moments later they had disappeared into the violet dusk and Jaguar, realizing suddenly just how tired he was, spread his ground sheet along the bottom of his hole and went to sleep almost at once. The trap was ready to be sprung.

CHAPTER 5

A thin mist writhed eerily over the surface of the river as they reined in their horses. In single file and absolute silence, the couple of hundred hand-picked Cossacks threaded their way to the edge of the Gaderbach. Bogdan, in the lead, moved softly into the water. It was warm and there was little current, as he had predicted. He waited till its level reached his chest, then holding his pistol above his head, he swam the rest of the way in a one-armed side stroke. Behind him the Cossacks had also begun to enter the slow-running water. Within minutes they were all across and were squelching in their water filled boots to the cover of the nearest willows.

'All right,' he whispered, 'move out — and I'll have the balls off any one who makes a noise. Follow me!'

The night was silent save for the steady croak of the frogs and the mysterious splashes of creatures in the water. Once what looked like a single star fell like a silver drop of light from the sky. But the flare was followed by an even inkier darkness. They had not been spotted. The long progress southwards continued.

A light wind started to blow. The young *sotnik*, who had killed the two Americans, suddenly laid his hand on the General's shoulder. Bogdan stopped instantly. 'What is it?' he whispered urgently.

Instead of answering, the *sotnik* pointed to their front. Bogdan could not see anything at first, but setting his eyes at an angle in the old Cossack fashion, he looked again. This time he saw what the keen-eyed *sotnik* had already spotted. A head dimly silhouetted against the skyline and behind it what appeared to be a crouching file of men.

He indicated that the *sotnik* and the leading four Cossacks should follow him. Noiselessly they moved forward, coming in at the crouched men's flank, knives and sabres already bared, ready for action.

They caught the partisans by complete surprise. One of them attempted to resist, but Bogdan's sabre flashed silver in the faint light and clove his skull in two.

Hastily the Italians, hands raised high above their heads, allowed themselves to be herded to some peasant's hut nearby.

To Bogdan's surprise it was occupied. An old crone stood there, trembling in every skinny limb, holding her claws of hands around two ragged barefoot children who were kneeling, hands clasped in supplication, the tears streaming down their frightened, emaciated faces. In the corner, an old, old man with a white thatch of hair, held his arm protectively around what appeared to be their only possession, a flea-bitten, shabby ancient donkey.

'Tell them we won't hurt them, *sotnik*,' Bogdan said to the captain, who spoke some Italian.

There were six of them, all clad in the blue beret and red scarf of the Communist partisans and all in their teens, save one whose pallid face, covered as if with grease, was contorted with sheer, unadulterated terror. That was the one who would sing, he told himself.

'*Sotnik*,' he snapped, 'ask the one who looks as if he's going to crap himself where the rest of his unit is located.'

The *sotnik* translated the General's question swiftly.

Lionheart gulped painfully, hardly able to breathe in his terror. 'I can ... cannot,' he gasped, twisting his head to one side, as if his collar were choking him, 'I cannot betray my comrades.'

'Kolchik,' Bogdan snapped. 'His right ear.'

Kolchik, a hulking Cossack with golden earrings in both ears, moved fast. His knife flashed. The Italians gasped. Next instant Lionheart howled with absolute agony, as his ear came off into the grinning Cossack's dirty hand.

'Don't think he'll need that ear pierced for a ring anymore, General,' Kolchik grunted and dropped it onto the floor. Lionheart, blubbering like a small child, stared down at the piece of flesh in amazement.

'Hold your water,' the *sotnik* bellowed. 'Now speak, if you don't want to lose your other ear.'

This time Lionheart did not refuse. 'They're dug in on the river south of here, just above San Vigilo,' he gasped hurriedly, holding up his blood stained hands in front of his contorted face, as if to ward off a new attack.

Bogdan ignored the restlessness of the partisans. Lionheart was singing. He had to get the information he needed quickly before they moved on. 'Ask him what their strength is and whether they've got any heavy weapons — mortars, mgs, artillery.'

The answer was to Bogdan's satisfaction. The partisans' heaviest weapons were their machine guns. '*Horoscho*,' he exclaimed delightedly. 'Good!'

'What about the macaronis, General?' Kolchik asked expectantly, feeling his knife with his thumb.

In other circumstances, Bogdan would have ordered the instant execution of the partisans — he had no time for communists. But he reasoned that if they were found murdered near the peasant's cottage, the pathetic scarecrows would be the ones to suffer the partisans' revenge. 'No, you big rogue, not this time. We'll tie them up and leave them here.'

Outside, while they waited for the Cossacks to tie up the partisans, Bogdan's gaze fell on the faded scrawl painted on the cottage's wall. 'What does that mean, *sotnik*?' he asked idly.

With some difficulty the keen-eyed captain translated the faded letters. 'Only God … can bend the Fascist will — men and things never!'

'By the Holy Virgin of Kazan,' Bogdan cursed, 'that on the wall of this place! What hypocrisy!' With a curse, he took out another packet of German cigarettes and tossed them into the pathetic hovel.

Among the bushes and willows which lined the bank, the frogs and cicadas which had croaked and clicked all night had fallen silent at last. From his forward observation post, Jaguar watched the Russians going about their morning tasks. A woman in a blue and white striped dress kneeled devotedly at one of the fresh graves where they had buried the dead the night before. A long line of men sat grumpily on a log supported by two boxes over the latrine trench. A couple of men in the black *cherkasskas* of Cossack officers, bejewelled daggers stuck in their belts, black fur caps thrust to the backs of the heads in a jaunty manner, surveyed the river, as if they were considering which would be the best spot at which to ford it.

It was obvious the Cossacks did not suspect the presence of the partisans and would be soon moving across the water, straight into the trap that was prepared.

'Alcohol's bad for you, Half-a-Gun,' Jaguar quipped to his Second in Command, who had his long nose buried in a canteen of red wine. 'Besides I think you're too young to be already drinking in the morning.'

Half-a-Gun looked up, his lips red with wine. 'Comrade Commander, you are full of shit — with permission.'

Jaguar grinned. 'What news of Comrade — er — Lionheart?'

Half-a-Gun shrugged carelessly. 'That particular bastard has not yet appeared, Comrade Commander. Probably he is busy writing his memoirs — or hiding in the nearest barn till the shooting is over —'

'Comrade Commander!' an urgent voice interrupted the boy's words. Jaguar swung round. A young partisan was standing there, gesturing wildly. 'Some of them are moving off — southwards.'

'*Southwards?*' Jaguar echoed. 'But they can't. They're supposed to cross the river here.'

'Look for yourself, Comrade Commander,' the young partisan replied.

Jaguar's eyes followed the direction of the partisan's outstretched arm. The man was right. Perhaps four or five hundred of the Cossacks were trotting slowly along the opposite bank, eyes fixed to their front, obviously showing no interest in the crossing point covered by the hidden partisans.

'What are they up to?' Half-a-Gun asked.

'I'll tell you,' Jaguar replied bitterly. 'They're smarter than we thought. They're throwing out a flank guard, which will cross the river further down to cover the main crossing — and look!' He pointed to another group of mounted Cossacks which was beginning to trot easily to the north. 'That's the northern flank guard. When they're in position, the main body with the wagon train will cross here opposite us.'

'So if we hit the main body, those bastards to north and south will give us hell.'

'Right,' Jaguar answered bitterly. 'All our efforts have been for nothing.'

'No, they haven't, Comrade,' the youngster answered. 'If we divide up the battalion and stop those two flank guards, we'll still be able to hit the main body when they cross with the machine guns.'

'Of course, you're right, the Spandau's will reach up to 800 metres accurately.' Swiftly, Jaguar changed his plan.

'Half-a-Gun, you take the First and Second Companies and cover those bastards to the north. I'll take the two remaining companies and do the same in the south. At the double!'

'At the double, Comrade Commander!' Half-a-Gun began to rap out his order. Minutes later the partisan battalion was split into two, hurrying out of their well-sited slit trenches to take up their new positions, exactly as a watching General Bogdan had anticipated they would.

CHAPTER 6

Intently General Bogdan studied the back of the head of the boy he was about to kill. His jet-black hair was too long for a soldier's and set in a thick mass of curls right down to the nape of the skinny neck.

The Cossacks were crouched in a grove of trees only a hundred metres from the partisans who had formed a rough skirmish-line in the willows on the river bank, waiting expectantly for the Cossacks to begin their crossing. Now they had no time to dig themselves in as they had done in their former position; now they made a perfect target for the men, who unknown to them, were concealed to their rear.

Bogdan waited for Boris' signal. Around him his young Cossacks, their broad, bold faces grimmer than usual, clutched their knives and sabres in hands that were beginning to sweat. The day grew hotter.

Suddenly the oppressive silence was broken by a shrill whistle. Boris' signal. His Cossack squadrons would now attempt their feint river crossing.

Now the morning was full of the sound of horses galloping into the water, the cries of Cossacks surging forward to the assault and above them the urgent commands of the teenage partisan in charge of the men lining the bank. Abruptly the line erupted into violent action. Bogdan rose to his full height and shouted. '*Cossacks — to the charge!*'

The trapped partisans swung round. 'Treachery!' their leader yelled, his machine pistol chattering crazily. A couple of Cossacks running next to Bogdan skidded to a sudden stop and fell heavy in the steaming grass. Kolchik raised his long knife. The wicked blade glinted in the sun a deadly silver as it hissed through the air. It struck Half-a-Gun in the centre of his narrow chest. He screamed piteously and sank to his knees, his finger still crooked around the trigger, but his bullets flying purposelessly into the sky. Next instant a Cossack boot crashed into the side of his head and he went down without another sound. The bank of the river was transformed instantaneously in a frantic chaotic scene of mayhem and bloody murder.

Bogdan grasped the boy's neck. The partisan screamed hysterically but Bogdan had no mercy. He exerted ever more pressure, bending his own head backwards so that he could use all his strength. Suddenly something gave within the boy. Like a broken doll, he sagged limply in Bogdan's grasp, all life gone from him. Bogdan lowered him to the grass, not daring to look at that dreadful face with its protruding purple tongue and frantic bulging eyes.

In that same moment, a crazy zig-zag of tracer fire hissed by his head. He ducked instinctively feeling the hot lead burn on his cheek as it flew past. Less than six metres away an olive-skinned boy raised a machine pistol and took more careful aim. This time he wouldn't miss. Bogdan's hand reached for the knife in his boot. It was gone! He must have lost it in the charge. With a sudden sinking feeling, he realized it was all over at last — and he was glad. Slowly he raised himself to his full height, his massive chest thrown out almost proudly, ready to die like a Black Cossack should.

At the same moment Major Boris spurred his horse up the bank and charged full tilt at the unsuspecting partisan. At the last moment he turned. Too late! Boris's sabre flashed. The youth caught one last glimpse of a great dripping horse, a horrifying lobster-pink face and the thin artifical lips drawn back over steel, foam-flecked teeth. Then the silver sabre came searing down on his defenceless head, cutting through the blue-beret, which flushed a sudden scarlet, into the skull and deep into the head so that abruptly the youth had two faces. Without a sound, he dropped to the ground and Boris's sabre came out with a sucking noise, its blade a bright scarlet.

Boris reined in his horse and looked down at the General 'You owe me a life, General.'

'I'll remember, Boris,' Bogdan grinned back. 'Now stop this mess. We need what's left of them.'

'*Horoscho*!' Boris tugged at the bit so that his mare reared high into the air on its hindlegs with sudden pain. 'Stop,' he cried in Italian. 'Stop, do you hear!'

Gradually the firing, the crying, the slaughter died away, leaving behind no sound save the moans of the wounded and an echoing silence that seemed to last for an eternity.

'Comrade Commander!' the partisan called urgently.

'What is it?' Jaguar snapped angrily, not taking his eyes off the Cossack cavalry massing on the other bank, as if about to attempt a crossing at any moment.

'To our rear.'

'What about it?'

'There's something strange going on, Comrade Commander.'

Alarmed by the tone of the other man's voice, the Jaguar swung round and caught his breath with surprise. A weary, ragged line of partisans were advancing on their positions. 'Why, they're Half-a-Gun's com —' He stopped short, as he saw the fur-capped horsemen herding their prisoners forward in front of them, cracking their long black knouts across their backs whenever they seemed to be advancing too slowly.

'*Prigionieri*!'

'*Si, si*,' Jaguar rapped.

'What are we going to do, Comrade Commander?' the other man quavered, as more and more of the partisans turned to stare in awe at the strange, silent advance on their positions.

Jaguar swallowed hard and raised his long-barrelled 9mm Glisenti automatic.

'Comrade Commander,' the partisan crouching next to him, cried in horror, 'they are our comrades!'

'We mustn't let that get in our way,' Jaguar said thickly, feeling his throat flood with hot sickening bile.

The partisan recoiled in horror. 'But our comrades…'

Jaguar took aim at the big man in officer's uniform riding on a white horse at the centre of the beaten, forlorn prisoners. In that same moment, his eyes fell on the pallid partisan in front of the horseman, trying to keep in his intestines, pulsating in his bloody hands like a nest of snakes. It was Pietro Gambetti, who had been with him from the beginning, the author of the Brigade's first password in the black days of 1944: 'The way to the mountains is the way to glory.'

Slowly, very slowly, he began to lower his pistol; he couldn't shoot Pietro! His men looked at him expectantly, wondering what they should do. In disgust Jaguar tossed the Glisenti into the grass and rose to his feet. 'We surrender,' he said, not daring to look at their pale young faces. And when they didn't move quickly enough for him, he cried angrily, 'Didn't you hear what I said, damn you? We surrender! Throw down your weapons and get to your dirty feet! They've won, damn you!'

Reluctantly the partisans tossed their weapons into the grass and rising to their feet, placed their hands on their blue berets in the gesture of surrender. Swiftly the officer on the white stallion and a companion galloped towards the downcast partisans.

With a flourish and in a cloud of dust the two of them reined in their sweat lathered horses in front of the partisan position and Jaguar recognized in the harshly handsome face of the Cossack leader, a man of indomitable will.

Bogdan glanced along the downcast line of partisans and said to the *sotnik*: 'Ask them who is their commander?'

'I am the commander. We do not wear badges of rank in the Garibaldi,' Jaguar replied in Russian.

Bogdan looked down at the young man with the high intellectual forehead, 'You speak Russian?' he said.

'Yes, I learned it in Moscow — at the Frunse Academy — before the war.'

For a moment Bogdan looked at the Italian appraisingly. 'So you're one of them, eh?' he said, 'a trained agitator?'

Jaguar thrust out his thin chest proudly. 'Not an agitator, General, but a communist leader.'

Bogdan grinned easily. 'Well, my fine young communist, I also was one of you once. And what did it get me?' His face darkened suddenly, 'Disgrace, imprisonment, the loss of my wife and child. That was my reward for serving Moscow loyally for twenty years and shedding my blood for that Georgian monster, Stalin.'

Jaguar fought back his rage at the insult to the great Russian leader; he knew that their lives depended upon his keeping control of himself. 'I know nothing about that,' he snapped. 'What is it you want of me?'

Bogdan shrugged carelessly. 'I want nothing of you *comrade*. I can dispose of you like that,' he clicked his thumb and forefinger together loudly. 'Your lives are in my hands. Your question should be — how can we save ourselves?' He leaned forward over the mane of the big white horse. 'I shall tell you how. We are moving north to the mountains. They tell me —

comrade — that the area is infested with partisans. Now my Cossacks have been fighting for too long. So, I am prepared to make a deal with you — *comrade.*'

In spite of his iron control, Jaguar felt himself flushing at the big Cossack's cynical use of the word 'comrade'. 'And what is that deal?'

'So that my men do not have to fight any more, I want to pass through the partisan area peacefully — and we have no quarrel with the Italians whatever their perverted political opinions might be. You and your men will ensure that we are not involved in any fighting.'

The proposition surprised Jaguar. 'How?'

'You will be our hostages until we reach the mountains. Once there we will turn you loose — on my word as a Cossack.'

'You mean whenever you might meet any of our comrades, our lives will guarantee your safe passage?'

'Exactly.'

'That is monstrous,' Jaguar exploded. 'I can't allow you … you war criminals to get away with it. Traitors to your own country, hired fascist killers…' The words died away as the big Cossack rose in his saddle and raised his pistol. 'This is the alternative.' He aimed at Pietro and fired at the same moment.

Pietro screamed shrilly. His hands fanned the air. Next moment he fell flat on his face, dead.

'You bastard!' Jaguar cried.

Bogdan remained unmoved. 'It's the lives of my men against those of yours,' he said coldly, replacing his pistol in the black holster. 'I will have no compunction about shooting the bunch of you, if you don't do as I wish.'

Jaguar let his shoulders slump in defeat. In spite of his principles, he could not let his men be slaughtered in cold blood. 'All right,' he said through gritted teeth. 'We'll play your little game for you, Cossack. But I promise you this.' Suddenly his liquid eyes flashed with hate. 'If I ever catch you off guard, I'll slit your throat'

Bogdan grinned easily. 'You have my permission to do so, if you ever do catch me off my guard — *comrade*.'

CHAPTER 7

All that 1 May, 1945, they moved north. The day was furnace hot. The Cossacks enviously eyed the cool snow-bound peaks in the far, far distance, as they plodded relentlessly forward, their horses' heads drooping wearily, their flanks gleaming with sweat.

In spite of the burning rage and humiliation that he bore within him, Jaguar could not help but admire these bold Russians, who had been written off by history, but who were yet trying to create a new life for themselves. He could not conceal his admiration for their leader either. The man was tireless. He was here, there and everywhere, cajoling, threatening, encouraging, not hesitating to use his black knout on laggards.

The hours passed. They rode by a squadron of black uniformed Fascist militia with the plumed side-hat of the Bersaglieri, tears streaming down their bitter faces as they systematically smashed their transport under the cold eyes of a grizzled captain, his chest ablaze with the ribbons of a quarter of a century of campaigning. Tyres were slashed, radiators smashed under the blows of a sledge-hammer, gear levers kicked off, fuel tanks holed with bursts of machine pistol fire.

Jaguar hated these men. He had fought them yet they were Italian and in their moment of utter defeat, he could not bear to see the look of their weeping faces. He turned his head away. Bogdan didn't. He had known the bitterness of defeat often enough in the past. It could be neither mocked nor overlooked. As he rode past the little grizzled Bersaglieri Captain, he lifted his hand and gave him an immaculate salute.

The Italian clicked to attention and returned the salute, as if he was still in that triumphant battalion which had goose-stepped down the Via del' Impero on their return from Abyssinia and Mussolini had cried to the cheering throng, his voice rich and vibrant through the amplifiers, 'Blackshirts of the revolution, Italian men and women, at home and throughout the world, hear me... Italy has at last her Empire ... a Fascist Empire!'

Towards evening they came across a column of burning German carts, abandoned by their drivers after the Allied dive-bombers had shot up the convoy.

'In God's name,' Bogdan cried in horror when he saw the German drivers had not stopped to free the horses in their panic. 'They are roasting alive in the shafts there. Follow me!'

The ammunition cart was aflame at the rear. The nag pulling it was desperate with fright, quivering violently, its eyes wild with fear. Bogdan sliced through the nearest trace with one sweep of his sabre. Behind him tracer ammunition started to explode in the cart, zig-zagging straight up into the hard, blue sky. Fearlessly Bogdan ducked under the horse and sliced through the other trace. Swiftly he grabbed its mane and dragged it out of the traces, fiery sparks flying everywhere. In the same moment the ammunition exploded in one great crash, throwing him on his back.

With the sparks still flying from his uniform, Bogdan staggered to his feet and ran to the next horse, a crazed chestnut, screaming piteously as it burnt, still attached by steel harness to a charred cart. He didn't hesitate. His sabre swept through the air and cut deep into the horse's neck. The hideous primeval screaming came to a sudden end.

And then it was all over and the only sound the dry crack of the Cossacks' revolvers as they shot the horses too grievously hurt to be saved; and Jaguar was left staring at the bare-headed General in his singed black coat in wonder.

That long May day while the Cossack trek moved slowly towards the glistening mountains, tremendous events were taking place elsewhere which would determine the fate of the Black Cossacks. In far-off Flensburg, Admiral Dönitz received the penultimate telegram from the besieged German forces in Berlin. It read: 'Führer died yesterday 1530 hours. In his will dated 29 April, he appoints you as president of the Reich... Form and timing of announcement to the Armed Forces and the public is left to your discretion. Acknowledge.' A little later, Hamburg Radio, following the slow movement from Bruckner's Seventh Symphony, announced: 'Our Führer, Adolf Hitler, fighting to the last breath against Bolshevism, fell for Germany this afternoon.'

But already the German fronts to the west, east and south were crumbling away rapidly, unable to withstand the pressure on all sides exerted by a whole host of nations, allied in a strange coalition against Germany, now motivated solely by a common hate and no longer a common purpose.

That afternoon a British field-marshal, Alexander, radioed an SS General, who had once been Himmler's personal aide, Wolff, asking whether the secret armistice, surrendering the enemy armies in Italy which had been agreed upon between the two men, would still take place on the following day.

All that long afternoon, the silver-haired urban SS General tried to persuade his fellow commanders to agree. Man after man disagreed with him. In exasperation, he cried: 'Look here, don't waste any more time. It's Germany that's at stake and not individuals. Please see this thing through with me. Tell the

Army commanders that the orders for surrender are to be strictly carried out.'

That night Field-Marshal Kesselring, the head of the German forces in the West, telephoned Wolff in a tremendous rage. 'How dare you act on your own without orders?' he shouted over the phone from Germany.

Wolff reminded the crimson-faced Air Force Field-Marshal that he had known about the surrender negotiations all the time. 'If you'd joined us then,' he barked, 'a lot of human blood need not have flowed and a great deal of destruction could have been avoided. You'll do well to follow my advice. You don't seem to realize what's at stake.'

Kesselring interrupted, excited now and no longer angry. 'You mean you made a deal with the Anglo-Americans to join in the fight against Tito and Russia?'

'*Herr Generalfeldmarschall,*' Wolff exclaimed in disgust, 'I don't know where you get such ideas. The Allies are not going to fight Russia. The war's over. I've negotiated a simple military surrender and I've managed to save a lot of our men. They won't go to Siberia or North Africa or God knows where else, and I could probably do the same for many of the others if I had a chance. Particularly now that the Führer's death has become known and you, too, are released from your oaths, it's your duty to refuse to transfer this oath of allegiance to anyone else. No oath of personal loyalty is transferable anyway. I'm not in the least interested in *Grossadmiral* Dönitz. I feel in no way bound to him. He means less than nothing to me. Whoever goes on fighting now is nothing but a war criminal'

Kesselring ranted and roared for a while longer, then he gave in. 'All right, Wolff,' he said, 'surrender it is. Deliver us into the victors' hands. Let's only hope they will be generous with us.' The phone clicked and went dead in Wolff's hands.

General Mark Clark received the news that night from Alexander, after he had already retired. Immediately he got up, and still in his pyjamas, went into action. Aides ran back and forth from his bedroom, bearing messages and orders to his diverse forces, British, Canadians, Brazilian, French, Moroccan, American. Hastily he prepared a press handout to be released to the press as soon as the surrender came into force, 'Fighting has ceased in Northern Italy west of the Izonzo river with the unconditional surrender of all enemy troops under command of German Army Group 'C'. There remains only the multitudinous administrative details of assembling and disarming the scattered and disorganized remnants of the once proud *Wehrmacht*.'

'Brother and that is certainly no bull,' Clark breathed, as he dismissed the stenographer who had taken down the message. 'But Bill, we've got to make it quick through those Krauts up there to stake out as much of Austria as we can. And don't forget to ensure that the press boys get the details of how many prisoners-of-war the Fifth Army takes as soon as we've got them.'

Brigadier-General McMahon smiled to himself, aware of just how important publicity and newspaper headlines were to the Commanding General. But they were all the same — Eisenhower, MacArthur, Patton and all the rest of them — they sulked like Hollywood movie stars if they were not in the headlines back home every morning. He told himself that there had never been a war like this, with the film camera and the news reporter looking over a general's shoulder all the time. 'What about the Russkis, sir?' he asked. 'That Colonel Serov has been giving me a hard time again?'

'That jerk. I'd like to give him a kick up his big heavy Russian ass! Tell him I'm having General Kislenko from the Allied

Commission to go up to Bolzano to sign the surrender document tomorrow.'

'And the Cossacks?'

'What Cossacks?' Clark queried, his mind elsewhere.

'Those renegade Russians who have been fighting for the Krauts. You ordered the Tenth to take them out. You'd promised their General's head on a silver platter to Serov, if I remember correctly, sir.'

'Did I? Where are they now, Bill?'

'According to our latest info, sir, they're heading northeast from Bolzano in the direction of Tolmezzo.'

'Isn't that just below Lienz?'

'Yessir.'

Clark beamed suddenly, relieved that his men wouldn't have to waste time on a dirty situation which would bring very unfavourable headlines. 'That's the area the British are going to take over, Bill. So let's call off the Tenth Mountain and let the Limeys have a crack at our Russian friends.' He smiled craggily at his Deputy Chief. 'After all the Limeys have had a couple of centuries' experience of dealing with uppity natives. From now on it's their pigeon. Now, about that surrender photo session with the press corps tomorrow...'

CHAPTER 8

'*Voina kaputt*,' the Cossacks cried joyously when they received the news on their looted civilian radios on the evening of 2 May. '*Viona kaputt*!' Immediately the Cossack camp was in an uproar. Cossacks proceeded to get blind drunk in the traditional fashion of their nation, drinking the fiery spirit straight from enamel pails.

Those who spoke other languages tuned into foreign stations and listened at full blast to the blare of noise, happy voices, hooting horns in the Western World's capitals as the foreigners celebrated the beginning of the end. Far away in the plain, the Americans celebrated too and watched flares and star shells zig-zagging through the sky as they marked the end of the two year slog up the boot of Italy. To the north, however, where the Germans lay, fires were glowing too. But there was nothing happy about them. They seemed ghost fires, lit to burn away the guilty evidence of the past. Even their Italian prisoners celebrated in their own way, shaking each other's hands and embracing fervently, repeating the same word over and over again, as if it had some magical significance '*finito … finito…*'

General Alexei Bogdan was not moved. Moodily he drank his vodka in the command tent with Boris. Finally Boris broke the gloom of the little baking hot tent by asking: 'What now, General?'

Bogdan looked at him almost sullenly. 'What do you mean — what now?'

'I mean, General, what are we going to do? How does the surrender of the Fritz Army affect us?'

'Well, the Fritzes are finished. They no longer can control, or protect us. Now, sooner or later, we will come under the control and protection of the Anglo-Americans.'

'You say protection, General,' Boris said, looking worried.

'Yes. You see, Boris, the question now is how far will the Anglo-Americans go to assist their Red allies in our matter. Will they protect us?'

'Our matter?'

'You see there are about 600,000 of us, from every republic of the USSR, who bore arms against the Reds for the Fritzes. How many of us will end up in Western Allied hands.' He downed another vodka in a quick gulp and pulled a wry face. 'Will the Anglo-Americans hand all those men back to the Reds if they know what will happen to them once they have passed into the Russian lines?'

'But that would be mass murder, General,' Boris protested hotly. 'They wouldn't do that!'

Bogdan shrugged. 'I just don't know, Boris. But what I do know is this. We shall continue our march north. Once we are in those mountains they will have their hands full in any attempt to root us out. If we can survive up there for six months, then I think things will have changed. Once the Anglo-Americans begin to live cheek by jowl with the Reds, they'll soon discover what their true intentions are. Perhaps then *they* will realize they need the services of the Black Cossacks too, just as the Fritzes did.'

Boris brightened up. 'Of course, sir! Who knows how to fight the Reds better than us? They'll need us sure enough in due course. In the meantime we'll find us a good place in the mountains, with plenty of vodka and perhaps some of those big-bosomed macaroni wenches!'

For a long time, Bogdan could not sleep. He tossed and turned in the stuffy little tent, thinking of everything that had happened to him in this long cruel war, which was now over: how the German agents had rescued him from the Red concentration camp; how he had formed the Black Cossack Division from a bunch of Cossack outlaws living wild in the Caucasus mountains; how they had fought battle after battle for their German masters until he had finally realized that not only had the Fritzes betrayed him and his people but also that they would never return to their Quiet Don. They would never create a new Cossackia on the banks of the great river which ran through their lost homeland, as the German agents had promised them. Now he and his Cossacks were condemned to be exiles for the rest of their lives like their forefathers before them.

Once he got up and lighting the lantern, poured himself half a tumbler of vodka so that he might sleep. He caught a glimpse of his face in the shaving mirror. It was hard and hollowed out, the face of a man who had been burdened too early with too many responsibilities: the face of a general.

He flung himself back into his bunk. Outside the noise of the carousing Cossacks was beginning to die away now. He closed his eyes. Could he pull it off — the new task he had set for the Division? In the darkness, his jaw hardened in determination. Of course, he could! He had done it in the past; he could do it again. He had to!

But General Alexei Bogdan was not fated to sleep till morning, in spite of the last half tumbler of vodka. At about three when the camp was bathed in sleep, Bogdan was awakened by a noise. He was alert immediately, every sense functioning as he tried to locate the sound. Then he had it. Something — or someone — was attempting to get under the canvas of the tent!

Swiftly he reached under the blanket for his pistol. He clicked off the safety catch and waited. A dark shape came under the canvas. Bogdan caught a quick gleam of silver. The intruder was armed with a knife. Just as the dark figure straightened up, Bogdan called: '*Stoi*!'

'It's me, General!' the dark figure called back in Russian.

It was the Italian partisan leader.

'What do you want?' he demanded.

'To kill you,' Jaguar cried and launched himself forward in the same moment.

BOOM!

A scarlet flash stabbed the darkness. But Bogdan had missed and a second later, Jaguar's lithe body landed on top of him in the bunk. He grunted and instinctively raised the hand clutching the pistol. He yelped with pain as Jaguar's knife stabbed into his wris.t The pistol fell from his wounded hand and clattered to the floor.

Immediately Bogdan's muscles coiled like a snake's. His wounded arm held in front of his chest protectively to parry any attempt to stab him in the chest, he sought the Italian with the other hand.

Jaguar was quicker. He stabbed downwards. Bogdan caught the flash of the knife. Just in time he moved his head to one side. The knife stabbed into the blanket. In one violent corkscrew movement, Bogdan twisted round and with his good hand caught the Italian's nearest thumb. Jaguar screamed with agony as Bogdan twisted it cruelly. The knife fell from his hand. He jerked his free elbow backwards. It caught Bogdan under the nose. Bogdan felt hot blood flood his face. Instinctively he relaxed his hold. Jaguar seized his chance. His hands sought and found Bogdan's throat. He cried an oath in Italian and exerted all his strength.

In the darkness, Bogdan, choking for breath, caught a frantic glimpse of Jaguar's contorted face. Slowly, agonizingly, Bogdan prepared to release himself from that terrible, killing grip. He fought to free himself of the blanket which trapped his legs. Then he'd done it. With red stars exploding crazily in front of his eyes and a great roaring wind threatening to burst his eardrums, he brought his knee up blindly into the Italian's crotch.

Jaguar screamed, a terrible gurgling yell and crashed to the floor, just as the first sentry flung open the tent flap and flashed his torch inside at the man writhing and moaning back and forth on the floor, his knees drawn up in unbearable agony.

Bogdan lay on his bunk and panted through clenched teeth, his wounded hand held out while Boris poured vodka into the knife gash. He blinked his eyes a couple of times to rid them of the tears of pain. Then he looked at the skinny partisan who was now recovering though there were still traces of vomit in his jet black beard. He swallowed hard and said, 'I thought the war was over, *comrade*?'

'Not for you, General,' he answered slowly and thickly.

'What do you mean?' Bogdan winced as Boris poured another dose of vodka into the wound.

Jaguar gave him a hang-dog look. 'Where do you think you and your traitors are going to?' he said boldly enough all the same. 'There is nowhere for you now. You have come to the end of the road, General. Every man's hand is against you. You may hide yourselves in the far mountains for a little while longer and then they'll come looking for you. You can be sure of that, General Alexei Bogdan.'

Bogdan tore his arm away from Boris's grasp angrily. The Macaroni was putting his own most dire thoughts into words. 'And you can be sure of this, *comrade*. You'll never see another dawn ... Guard,' he snapped to the burly Cossack guarding the Italian, 'take this man outside and deal with him.'

'Yes, General.' The Cossack grabbed at Jaguar's arm. 'Come on, spaghetti-eater, out with you.'

Jaguar let himself be taken, but at the flap to the tent, he paused and spat vindictively on the floor at Bogdan's feet. 'Let your end be more ignoble than this!' he cried and disappeared. A moment later there was a short dry burst of machine pistol fire outside, followed by a solitary cry and then silence. Bogdan looked at Boris but said nothing. He couldn't. What had just happened was a bad omen; it seemed a bad augury for the first day of peace.

CHAPTER 9

On the evening of the 3rd, the Black Cossacks crossed the River Tagliamento just east of the town of Tolmezzo and began the steep climb into the *Karnische Alpen*, which formed the border with Austria. They travelled all night, eager to get deep into the mountains before the Allied planes discovered them. Just before dawn Bogdan ordered them off the second-class road leading to the frontier at the small town of Arta, which seemed completely deserted. Bearing north-east, with the River Tagliamento to their right, feeling the air getting colder and colder as they climbed, they headed for Paulero, the last village on the Italian side before Austria.

From the map Bogdan knew there was water there and the young *sotnik*, who spoke Italian, had informed him that as Paulero was a mountain village, its population would be German-speaking South Tyrolean's, in spite of the Italian-sounding name of the place. Bogdan thought it a good sign. He knew from his months in Italy that the South Tyrolean's hated the Italians, who had taken them over from Austria after the First War. They would probably not object as much to the Cossacks' presence as Italians would. But whether the village was occupied by troops, German or Italians, he didn't know. He would find that out at dawn, when they reached Paulero.

The sun struck across the valley slantwise, throwing the little group of red-roofed, white-walled houses into stark relief. There was no movement save the silver leaves of the olive trees rustling in the slight breeze and no noise save the dawn chatter of the myriad birds in the trees around them.

'What do you think?' Bogdan asked, lowering his glasses for a moment, but keeping his hand over their lenses to avoid the light reflecting in them. 'Doesn't look as if the place is inhabited, does —' He stopped short, as Boris waved his free hand urgently. 'What is it?' he asked and threw up his glasses again.

'Look at that house at two o'clock, sir,' Boris said quickly. Bogdan swung his binoculars round. A thin trickle of blue smoke was rising straight up into the hard blue of the dawn sky. 'Yes, I see. The question is by whom?'

Ten minutes later, while the bulk of the Division laboured ever closer to them, the two officers discovered who occupied this particular little village.

A giant ten-wheel armoured car, its metallic body glittering in the sun's rays, crawled slowly out of the place, its progress marked by silence on the part of the two hidden watchers. Finally it disappeared out of sight, but not before the two of them had spotted the double SS insignia painted in bright silver on its side.

'The Fritz SS!' Boris breathed.

Bogdan nodded his head grimly. It looked as if the war was not over after all.

The men of the little patrol were already shaking their heads as they scuttled back down the track, their weapons slung over the backs of the black, sweat-stained shirts. 'Bad?' Bogdan asked eagerly.

'Yessir,' the blond NCO in charge of the patrol answered. 'They're dug in all around the village — and they've got 88s too. We cornered an old farmer in a field on the other side of the village. As far as he knew the Fritzes are not going to surrender. They're going to stick it out up there and fight to the death, if they're attacked.'

Bogdan thanked the patrol and dismissing them, began to consider the situation with Boris, using the point of his sabre to sketch in a rough map in the dust at the side of the mountain road. 'Their guns are covering the road and the river here. And you can see anyone attacking up the road would be compressed by the steepness of the mountain face to the right and the drop to the river on the left.

'The village itself extends along the road running off to Paluzze, and we can assume that they've got other guns covering that point, with probably the big armoured car we saw linking up the two positions.'

Boris pulled a face. 'That doesn't give us much of a chance, General. There are the mountains; if we could get the men up there and come down between the two positions where the road branches off at a forty-five degree angle to Paluzze — here, General.'

'Yes, we could, but it would take us a devil of a time to get the men up and over that ridge. Cossacks are not the greatest of mountain troops. There is one route to the village which isn't guarded, or at least, so I hope.'

'What is it, sir?' Boris asked eagerly.

'The river, though naturally those Fritz 88s will cover it.'

'But sir, there are a lot of imponderables. How are we to advance up the river in the first place? Secondly you are probably right they won't have built positions on the river but all the same, those 88s are a terrible weapon, once they've ranged in.' He touched his face that bore the tell-tale scars.

'I agree with you, Boris. But to point one. We don't *advance* up the river, we *sail* up it. There's plenty of timber about. We make rafts and transport the men that way, landing at this spot

— here.' He scratched an 'X' in the dust just beyond the bend in the road that led to Paluzze. 'As for the guns. Well, we've got nothing we can tackle them with save our mortars, so we go in under the cover of darkness and if and when we're in position, we'll put in a feint attack up the road to keep the 88s occupied. I'll ask for volunteers. It'll be a suicide mission, of course, on that narrow road.'

'Beg permission to command the feint attack,' Boris snapped. Bogdan smiled softly and reaching out his big hand, put it on Boris's shoulder affectionately, 'No my friend, this time you don't volunteer. The war is over, remember; you've done more than enough fighting.'

Tears sprang into Boris's lidless eyes, permanently bloodshot from the burning Italian sun against which his pupils had no protection. 'I would like to go, sir. Those greenhorns who call themselves Cossack cavalrymen need an old head who was using the Baklanov trick when they were still crapping in their nappies.'

'Not this time, Boris,' Bogdan answered. 'This might well be the last battle of our lives, my friend, and you know what we Cossacks say of the last battle. The good and the experienced die in the last battle. But not you, my friend, not you.'

CHAPTER 10

'All right, push off now!' Bogdan commanded, glancing at the pale blur of their faces in the gloom over the river.

With a grunt, the young, brawny Cossack, former River Don boatman, thrust his pole against the bank and heaved. Next to him one of the Cossacks crowded apprehensively on the hastily built raft said, 'I joined the army, not the navy. So be careful, little brother.'

'Be happy, Cossack,' Bogdan said. 'Now the Black Cossacks have got a navy too.'

The raft was caught by the current and started to gather speed almost immediately. Swiftly and expertly the boatman pushed his way to the back of the raft and began to steer the ungainly craft. Behind them raft after raft, laden with heavily armed men, swung towards the centre of the swift-flowing River Tagliamento. They were on their way.

Like most Cossacks, Bogdan had no stomach for the water and to him it seemed the raft was rocking from side to side frighteningly. Desperately he fought back the bile in his throat. He would be glad when this particular little midnight cruise was over.

Faster and faster the rafts ran towards the little village, as the river surged through a narrow chasm, its water heaving and leaping white in the darkness. But the Don boatmen saved their rough craft from disaster time and time again, fending off half-submerged rocks, steering away from sudden bends in the course of the river, riding the furiously boiling water expertly.

Just when the pale gleam ahead indicated they were almost out of the narrow rock chasm, a tremendous crash rang out.

Bogdan swung round. A raft had smashed into a submerged rock and dark bobbing heads struggled frantically in the wild water, burdened as they were with their heavy equipment. Bogdan crossed himself hastily and said a silent prayer that they would make it to the bank. Then turning, he concentrated once again on getting through this nightmarish midnight trip.

Gradually their speed lessened. Now the tense Cossacks could see the outline of the village above them to their left. But their attention was concentrated, not on the village, but the long sinister barrels of the three 88mm cannon pointing down the road along which the volunteers would attack at dawn.

If the SS spotted them now, it would be a massacre. Nothing happened. With his muscles rigid in tense anticipation, Bogdan watched the guns anxiously as the rafts moved underneath them at what seemed now an impossibly slow speed on the suddenly sluggish current. If the SS sentries at the gun pits were not asleep, then they certainly weren't looking in their direction.

Fifteen minutes later, the boatmen began to steer the waterlogged rafts out of mid-current and towards the dark, bush-fringed bank. The first phase of the operation had been successful

In the houses they had requisitioned from the peasants, the SS snored, unknowingly enjoying the last sleep they would have in this world. Faces set even in sleep, sleek yellow hair untidy on the rough pillows, they had come a long way to die in this remote Italian mountain village. Some of them had been in the war from the start: the lightning campaign against the Polish; the heady triumphant march through France in '40; the tremendous victories in Russia in '41 and '42; the murderous battles of the middle years of the war; then retreat, retreat,

retreat, with their numbers getting ever fewer, but ever tougher, hardened by the bitter, treacherous fighting of northern Italy, with every man's hand against them. Now there would be no more retreat for them. There could only be one fate for those who wore the double cross of the SS — *death*.

Bogdan stumbled forward through the waist-deep water which bellied against him. Behind him a small Cossack, carrying the barrel of one of their mortars almost disappeared into a pothole and was hauled to the surface cursing and spluttering, but still hanging on to the precious equipment.

Bogdan gave a final heave and pulled himself free of the water's grip and up the slippery bank. His eyes were now accustomed to the darkness, which seemed to shine with a kind of incandescence. All was still and silent. Their landing had obviously not been discovered. 'All right,' he called to the men waiting down below. 'Begin moving up now!'

Everywhere the Cossacks started to scramble up the muddy bank, cursing softly when they slipped. Within five minutes they were all assembled, some 300 men, plus a squad of machine gunners and mortarmen.

'Pass the word back, *sotnik*,' Bogdan whispered to the young captain, crouched behind him, 'move out now in battle order.'

'Battle order,' the word went from mouth to mouth.

Swiftly the Cossacks formed up into little squads on alternate sides of the little track that was the road to Paulero. Bogdan waited impatiently until they were ready, then he drew his sabre and flashed it in the direction of their objective. Phase two had begun.

At the guns covering the road from Arta, the sentries yawned wearily and lighting the last forbidden cigarettes of the night, told themselves that they would be stood-down soon. After all, the war was virtually over and the world had forgotten them in this remote corner of Italy.

As Corporal Heinz, the second in command of number three gun, remarked wearily to the gun-layer Spahn. 'The only thing that's wrong with this place, Spahn, is there's no nooky.'

The brilliant half ball of sun appeared above a bank of hazy violet cloud. The bright white light struck the parched heights with such force that the earth seemed to ring like metal under its impact. 'Here comes the fireman,' Spahn said.

'Yer,' Heinz agreed, 'here he comes — and it's going to be bloody hot!'

'You'll be able to get yer duds off, Corp and get your brittle ribs brown.'

'Yer,' Heinz said in disgust, 'and lie there with the sun bringing it to a boil, thinking of it and nothing to do but play with yourself —'

'Theme number one, I see,' Lieutenant Hart, the battery commander, broke into the tired pre-dawn conversation.

Automatically the two men snapped to attention, their cigarettes cupped in their right hands pressed stiffly to their sides.

'At ease, at ease.' Hart, a tall elegant officer, his right eye socket empty since the Battle of Kursk, covered by a black patch, waved them to stand at ease.

'Anything to report Heinz, you rogue?' he asked.

'Not a sausage, sir. As quiet as a knocking shop the day before payday.'

'Any sign of the enemy, sir?' Spahn ventured.

'The *late* enemy,' Hart corrected him. 'No, I think the Amis and Tommies have forgotten us. With a bit of luck they'll let us form the independent republic of Paulero. Then when the fuss and feathers about war crimes and all the rest of that pious nonsense is over, we might be able to slip back into the Homeland again.' Even as Hart said the words, he knew they were a lie. He touched his hand casually to his peaked cap, decorated with the tarnished silver death's head. 'Carry on, I'll stand you down in fifteen minutes and then you can get your heads down. It's going to be a hot day.'

After he had gone back to his Command Post, Spahn grunted, 'Not a bad bloke — for an officer, Hart. If anyone can get us back home, it'll be him.'

'Yer,' Heinz answered, but without much conviction. 'Hart'll pull it off.'

The sun beat down intolerably and as they marched to their start line, the single drooping telephone wire that connected the village with the outer world sang in the heat. From the vineyards to their right, the flies rose in swarms, attracted by the Cossacks' sweating bodies.

They passed a dead SS sentry, killed by the scouts, his own bayonet jutting from his bloodstained chest, flies already crawling over his unseeing eyes. Carefully each squad made a circuit round the dead body sprawled out in the dusty road. Someone in the last squad took out a dirty rag and dropped it over the man's face to keep the flies away from his eyes.

Just before seven that morning, they reached the tumbledown barn which was their start line. Its whitewashed walls threw back the morning light in a solid, blinding glare. Bogdan blinked his eyes rapidly, and crawling to a slit in the crumbling, loose-stone wall, peered out across the road into the village and up to the guns on the heights.

He could see every detail: the white circles around the long tapering barrels, which indicated the number of tanks their crews had knocked out; the big piles of 100 lb shells stacked neatly by each gun; the lazy sentries, dressed in summer khaki, but with their helmets camouflaged a mottled green in the SS fashion. He followed the contours of the height. The slope was pretty steep to their front, but not that steep. His Cossacks would be able to take it all right, as long as the gunners were occupied with the feint attack and kept their backs to them. But if they were caught out on that slope, it would be sheer bloody slaughter.

He looked at his watch. It was nearly zero hour. Now it was up to the volunteers of the feint attack. He slithered back into the barn. 'All right, you mortar crews, stand by, just in case. If anything goes wrong, it's up to you lot to give us some sort of covering fire.'

'Yes General,' Suslov, the mortar sergeant, a burly bearded veteran with one leg, snapped. He limped back to his crews. 'All right, you heard the General. I'll have the nuts off any one who makes a mess-up of this.'

This was going to be the very last time. They would never experience this moment, primed by danger, sensitive to every stealthy movement, attuned to a heightened awareness of the minutiae, the deadly minutiae of life around them, ever again. This was the last time!

CHAPTER 11

Beyond the height a flare hissed into the morning air. It hung there for an age, while the SS men around the gun stared up at it, eyes shielded against the sun, mouths open foolishly in surprise. In the same moment that it exploded above their heads, Corporal Heinz woke up to what was going on. 'Don't grow corns on your fat assess!' he yelled urgently. 'To the guns!'

The spell was broken. As the cavalry came five abreast round the bend, swinging their curved sabres, the SS men doubled frantically for the 88s. The Cossacks screamed their old battle cries, carried away by the sheer excitement of the charge.

A Spandau went into action. Animals howled. Horses skidded to a halt, going down on their knees in agony. Men screamed. Abruptly the Cossacks were going down on all sides. But still they kept on coming, while the sweating, frightened SS men whirled their wheels and dials frantically, trying to bring the guns to bear on the wild men galloping up the road towards them.

Corporal Heinz's gun fired first. There was a great ripping noise. Purple flame spouted from the 88mm. Flat and low, the HE shell exploded with a thick crump just above the leading horsemen. They disappeared in a cloud of black-grey smoke. When the smoke cleared there was only one Cossack still standing in the welter of mutilated horses and men, pouring blood out of his boot. Before the gun could fire again, he hopped quite calmly back to the cover of the bend.

Bogdan knew it was time to act. The first gun was already in action and it would be only seconds before the other two joined in. He drew his sabre and roared: '*Cossacks — to the attack!*'

'*Urrah!*' the guttural cry went up from 300 throats and the Cossacks charged forward. From the houses of the village, machine guns began to chatter. Cossacks went down but nothing seemed able to stop the fury of that charge. Grenades flew through the air. The SS machine gunners, dressed in their underclothes for they had been caught completely by surprise, were hurtled to the ground, where their heads were smashed in remorselessly by the butts of the Cossacks' rifles.

Within a matter of minutes the Cossacks had cleared the part of the village which led up to the height, leaving behind them a trail of their own dead and dying and those of the SS littering the bloodstained cobbled street. But Bogdan knew there was no time to waste. The SS gunners were still occupied with the suicide squad, but soon they would recognize the danger to their rear. He had to get up that height and deal with them before that happened.

Urgently he doubled forward, followed by his men, who in the usual Cossack fashion had stopped and begun to loot the dead bodies. A diabolic burst of high speed machine gun fire whipped just across his front, striking up a trail of blue-red sparks on the cobbles just in front of his feet. He skidded to a stop.

The big armoured car they had seen the night before crawled round the corner firing as it came. His heart sank. The damned thing barred the way to the heights. For a moment he stood there stupidly, paralysed by the enemy vehicle's sudden appearance. But as a second burst of fire hissed in his direction, he awoke to his danger. He ducked and in the same instant yelled above the racket, '*Suslov, the mortars!*'

The mortar sergeant hidden behind the barn saw the danger at once. 'Fire one, fire two,' he cried. 'Target armoured car, two o'clock!... *FIRE!*'

An instant later the ugly, fat-bellied black bombs were wobbling up into the burning sky. For a moment they seemed to be stationary as they reached the apex of their curve. Then they howled down at a tremendous speed. The first missed the armoured car by a dozen metres and shattered burning fragments against its sides. The second was right on target and the machine gunners flew high into the air, a tormented mass of broken, severed limbs. Abruptly the car came to a halt, thick white smoke pouring from its engine.

The squad next to Bogdan bolted forward, bodies low. The leading man flung a phosphorous grenade. It dropped in the centre of the dazed SS men and scattered fiery pellets of the deadly chemical on all sides.

Immediately the SS men started to scream, as the phosphorous began to burn on their flesh. But the Cossacks had no mercy. They fell on them as they rolled back and forth, chopping, hacking, slicing with their sabres and knives, until the SS men moved no longer and the bloody bodies could burn unhindered.

Bogdan seized his chance and ordered the charge. The Cossacks surged forward, their hearts reacting with excitement, caught up once again by the old blood-lust of battle.

Up on the heights the SS men were frantically attempting to swing round their deadly cannon to meet the new challenge. 'Sharpshooters,' Bogdan barked, running up the hill.

The keenest-eyed marksmen among the Cossacks dropped as one. Unslinging their rifles, they took rapid aim and began to pick off the gunners. Corporal Heinz went down, a neat hole drilled through the centre of his forehead punctuating the look of surprise on his face. Soldier Spahn yelped and clapping a hand to a suddenly lifeless shoulder, pitched face forward on to the grass. The veteran Hart reacted in the way a veteran should. He sprung up on the sand-bag parapet and fired quick controlled bursts from his machine pistol. Swinging the Schmeisser from left to right, his legs braced for the shock of what must come, he mowed down the massed ranks of the cheering Cossacks. Man after man tumbled to the ground so that those following stumbled and fell over their moaning, writhing bodies.

Then the sharpshooters concentrated their massed fire on the lone soldier outlined so clearly against the burning dawn. Hart was hit in the knee. He groaned with pain but continued firing. He was hit again in the shoulder. A terrible scream escaped his lips. Still he fired on. Then two slugs hit him squarely in the chest at the same time. He was bowled off the parapet as if punched by some gigantic fist. In that same instant the Cossacks, out for blood, swarmed over the parapet and into the gun crews. The SS dropped their shells and ramrods and fought for their lives. Bogdan waded through the confused mess of men and reaching the first 88, he extracted the firing pin from the breech block. He struck it with all his strength against the block itself. The pin smashed. He battled his way to the next 88. In a flash he had done the same there.

A dark-eyed burly German barred his way to the third. The man kicked out hard with his heavy nailed boot before Bogdan could react. He yelped with pain and dropped his sabre. He aimed a kick at the burly German's groin, but the German grabbed Bogdan's foot and twisted swiftly. Bogdan howled and went down. The German dived on to him, his big fingers grasping Bogdan's throat. But not for long.

'I think I owe you this, General!' Boris' voice cried. His sabre hissed. Next moment the German slumped limply over Bogdan, his hands still clasped around the General's neck, but his head missing. It lay neatly beside him on the grass staring at the headless body.

'Thank you, Boris. But didn't I tell you you weren't supposed to take part in the last action?'

Boris smiled, his mouth full of gleaming steel. 'I survived General, I survived and now it's all over.'

Half an hour later, it *was* all over. At the sight of a whole mounted Cossack regiment coming through the white painted houses towards them, the gunners manning the two 88s at the far end of the village panicked and all that was left for the Cossacks to do was to winkle out the few stubborn SS men, hidden in barns and behind the stone walls around the fields, who fought to the end. By midday on 4 May, 1945, the village of Paulero and the area between it and the main road leading to the Ploecken Pass was in the hands of the Black Cossacks. They could begin to establish their new Cossackia in this remote forgotten corner of Italy.

CHAPTER 12

During the following two days the Cossacks were busy establishing themselves in their new homeland.

Raiding parties rode out in the old Cossack fashion to seize women, food and drink. Suddenly the crude encampments they had set up in the olive groves and between the vineyards were filled with happy drunken Cossacks and protesting young Italian women, who soon calmed down when the half-wild young Cossacks had proved their virility.

Meanwhile Bogdan, who had billeted himself and his staff in the houses of the frightened villagers, tried to set up a new organization, halfway between a divisional command and a civilian administration. Permanent patrols of older Cossacks were established along all the approach roads and tracks to the village. The sole telephone line was cut so that effectively Paulero was sealed off from the outside world.

Next Bogdan called the village burgomaster, an ancient wrinkled *Weinbauer*, and explained to him what his plans for the village were.

His men would be strictly disciplined, once they had been allowed to indulge their cravings. He, Bogdan, would supply any extra labour the village needed to harvest their crop of olives and grapes.

Further, Bogdan explained, his Cossacks would not touch any property or any woman in the village itself. Any infringement would be punished most severely. At that the old burgomaster's leathery face cracked in a wicked smile, his faded eyes almost disappearing into the wrinkles. 'I don't know whether our womenfolk would be so happy about that,

General,' he said. 'You see, all our young men are in the German Army and our women haven't seen anything in trousers below the age of sixty for a very long time. I fear, General, you are committing a grave injustice there.'

With a grin, Bogdan dismissed the old burgomaster, feeling that he could work well with a man who possessed that kind of humour; it was almost Cossack.

On the afternoon of the 6th, he released his Italian prisoners and the handful of SS who had fallen into their hands alive. He would need them no more. Each man was given a hunk of bread, a bottle of water and a handful of virtually worthless Northern lire and sent on his way. The war was over. They would have to learn to live in peace with one another once more.

On that same evening, far, far away in the rainy Northern French town of Reims, Colonel-General Jodl of the *Wehrmacht*, who had come to plead for more time from the Allies to save his troops from the advancing Russians, told them: 'You'll soon be fighting the Russians yourselves. Save as many as you can for them.'

The Americans laughed in his face. In the end he gave in. He agreed to sign the unconditional surrender. He was escorted into the HQ's war room and with his face very pale, signed the agreement All German forces would surrender at 11.01 pm, 7 May, 1945.

Afterwards, on the verge of tears, he told the victorious generals assembled opposite him: 'With this signature the German people and German armed forces are, for better or worse, delivered into the victor's hands. In this war, which has lasted more than five years, both have achieved and suffered perhaps more than any other people in the world. In this hour,

I can only express the hope that the victor will treat them with generosity.'

But the pale-faced General, who would soon end on the gallows at Nuremberg, was mistaken in his hope. There was to be no sympathy for the Germans or those who had fought for them in the bitter vindictive months to come.

At that same hour, as the guns ceased firing all over Europe, silent at last after nearly six years, General Bogdan assembled his Cossacks for a *Krug*, a Cossack assembly. Their attention was fixed on the raised wooden platform from which the General would speak to them.

Finally with due ceremony, General Bogdan appeared mounted on his white stallion, his fur cap tilted at a rakish angle. At his side rode Boris, carrying the black flag of the Cossacks, acting as his aide in the old Cossack fashion.

The Cossacks clicked to attention. Bogdan raised his knout in acknowledgement, and with one easy movement sprang from Don and onto the platform.

'Cossacks,' he roared, his tremendous voice reaching even the rear ranks, 'I salute you!'

'General,' they yelled in red-faced unison, '*we* salute you!'

In the olive trees behind them the birds rose in alarm, squawking their hoarse protest at the sudden noise. Bogdan's harsh face suddenly softened in affection, like that of a proud father gazing fondly at his large brood. Then his look resumed its habitual fierceness: the aspect of a man fated to lead a nation. 'Cossacks,' he cried, 'we have come to the end of the road. We have been running and fighting for nearly four years now — and our forefathers were fighting and running from the Reds for twenty-odd years before that. Now we run no more!

'The fighting is over and we are exiled like our forefathers. But be not dismayed. We shall create a new Cossackia here in these mountains.' He raised his knout in warning. 'But do not expect it to be easy. We must learn to change our ways. The fighting days are over. We must learn how to become farmers again. You young men must learn that you can't take any woman you want. Those you've got, you keep.'

His sally was greeted by laughter and Boris, watching Bogdan, could almost feel in the very air how closely Bogdan and his men were attached to one another; they were his life and, in their turn, they would follow him to hell and back.

'One day, of course, the Anglo-Americans will find us up here. By that time we shall have established our Cossackia and have become peaceful farmers once again. Those of you who have women will have already begun to breed.' He clasped his big hands together, fingers intertwined. 'By then we shall have established roots up here and the Anglo-Americans will find us living in peace with our neighbours. Then I am sure they will pass on and leave us to live out our lives in this remote place. It is not our native earth, but Cossacks,' his voice hardened with repressed energy, 'we will make it our native earth!'

'We will, General!' they thundered back.

Bogdan nodded to Boris.

The Major handed him the tumbler of *grappa*. Bogdan raised it high so that all the assembled Cossacks could see it. 'Cossacks,' he bellowed, 'To our future!' In one gulp he drained it and next moment dashed the empty glass to the ground.

'To the future!' came the cry, drowning the low rumble of the thunder from the west, heralding the storm to come. '*TO THE FUTURE!*'

BOOK TWO: *THE BRITISH ARE COMING!*

CHAPTER 1

In the burning heat the Cossacks of von Pannwitz's 15th Cossack Cavalry Corps sweltered as the long line of British vehicles began to split up, the three ton trucks, which had come to bear them away, moving to the right, and the half-tracks, carrying the infantry, rattling to a stop in a cloud of thick white dust immediately to their front.

Stolidly and in total silence thousands of Cossacks, in their shabby field-grey German uniforms, watched as the British infantry in their scrubbed white equipment started to form up in front of them. The front rank was armed solely with white pickaxe handles, but the men of the two rear ranks carried rifles and were in full battle order, including steel helmets, as if they were going into action again.

For a few minutes the two groups of soldiers eyed one another: the veterans of the Eighth Army and the Cossacks. The silence was absolute as both sides tried to assess what the other would do: would they use force? Would they fight back?

Then suddenly the oppressive silence was broken by the shrill whistles of the platoon commanders, standing in front of each platoon of infantry. As one, the first rank started to advance on the expectant Cossacks, marching forward in perfect formation — they had practised the manoeuvre all the previous day. When they were a dozen yards from the Russian renegades, the whistles shrilled again and they halted in a cloud of dust. Immediately the infantry battalion's CO walked forward with the interpreter, a pudgy, bespectacled lance-corporal from the Pioneer Corps.

'Tell them, Corporal, that we are going to load them into the trucks peacefully. We will cause no trouble and we expect no trouble. Tell them that their fellow countrymen of the Red Army have promised that they will be treated fairly once they have crossed the demarcation line between them and the British Army at Judenburg. Tell them that.' He flicked away a fly with his swish and waited.

Swiftly the lance-corporal interpreted the colonel's words. But there was no response. The Cossacks preserved a stony silence. Someone brandished one of their black flags, decorated with a white skull and crossbones. That was all.

The young colonel, veteran of El Alamein, Mareth and the long, hard slog up the boot of Italy, bit his lip. In the last five years of total war, he had never been faced with a situation like this. But he knew he must act — and act decisively. After all the whole Battalion was watching him.

Without turning round, he barked, 'Front rank will advance and take them to the trucks.'

The platoon commanders blew their whistles. The soldiers gripped their pickaxe handles more firmly. As one they tramped forward, their lean brown faces suddenly hard and tense.

For the first time that morning the Cossacks reacted. From within their dense ranks, the old women and men began to wail, while like a herd of animals facing some terrible predator the rest edged ever closer together. The front rank of young, brawny men linked arms and went down on their knees. Abruptly they began to pray.

A young platoon commander grabbed hold of the shoulder of one of the kneeling men and tugged hard. The Cossack resisted. On both sides his comrades held on to him with all their strength. The platoons broke up into little groups, trying to prise out individual Cossacks in twos and threes. The whole crowd seemed to tremble and sway as the British infantrymen tried to remove the front-rank Cossacks. But to no avail.

Stronger measures were needed, if the officer were ever to get these damned Cossack renegades up to Judenburg. 'All right,' he bawled, 'move back the front rank!' He swung round to the waiting two rear ranks, their eyes full of a mixture of amusement and awe. Angrily, he gave the command he had not given since the Third Battle of Cassino a year before: '*Battalion will fix bayonets!*'

The colonel listened to the sound of the bayonets being fitted, judging exactly when his men were finished with the drill. 'Rear two ranks will advance,' he ordered, '*advance!*'

A low moan rose from the crowd. As the infantrymen, bayonets outstretched, started to advance upon them, the young Cossacks in the front rows ripped open their shirts and bared their chests, daring the Englishmen to plunge their bayonets in the naked flesh. Behind them, their fellows began to jeer at the grimly advancing troops.

'Take every fourth man,' the colonel ordered, his face angry and sweating now. 'No more messing with them now!'

Panic broke out everywhere. Men and women began to clamber over each other to get away from the British. Frantically the infantrymen tried to save the lives of those trapped beneath the struggling, screaming, panic-stricken mass. Wielding their pick-handles, digging and sticking with their bayonets, crashing down the brass-plated butts of their rifles on the mob, they tried to force the younger Cossacks to loosen their hold.

Vera Krasnova, struggling desperately to retain her hold on Lieutenant Pastryulin's slippery hand. A soldier crashed his butt down on Pastryulin's bare head. He shouted with pain, but he didn't let go. The soldier hit him again. Blood started to stream down the officer's head, blinding him. Vera began to feel his grip slackening. 'Hold tight Pastryulin,' she called desperately. 'Hold ti —' The Tommy, cursing furiously, rammed the butt of his rifle into the officer's face. Pastryulin let go.

In an instant Vera felt herself swept with the screaming, panicked mob of old men and women. She was pushed tight against the wall of one of the huts they had built when the Corps had first moved into this area of Austria. Screaming like the rest, she kicked and scratched, trying to free herself.

It was useless. Her beautiful young body was lifted high from the ground. Against her back, the window frame splintered and cracked. Her upper body fell back and her legs were impaled on the jagged shards of glass. Blood poured from the ragged wounds. Another heave and she was through, lying moaning and groaning on the dirt floor.

The British advance continued. Behind the crowd, a stout wooden fence splintered and burst. Screaming and clawing at one another to escape the soldiers, the Cossacks erupted through the sudden gap like lava from a volcano. Immediately they saw their chance. Desperately they scattered, running wildly for the cover of the fir forest beyond.

'Don't let them escape!' the colonel cried. 'The buggers are getting away with it!'

Vera Krasnova did not understand the words, but she understood their meaning well enough, as the soldiers followed the fleeing hordes. Moaning with pain, she staggered to her feet, knowing that this was her last chance. She flung open the door of the ruined hut. A Tommy tried to grab her, arms outstretched. She dodged him easily, running crazily for the gap and the woods beyond. Up ahead machine guns began to chatter, their fire wild and erratic. Cossacks scattered wildly for the cover of the trees as the white and red tracer zig-zagged through the forest.

Vera ran on, the bullets ploughing the earth all around her feet. She lost one shoe — then the other. Her speed increased. She flew through the trees, dodging from side to side wildly, as if the devil himself were after her.

She burst through a thick grove of firs, their twigs lashing cruelly at her flushed young face. She stopped dead. Before her lay a deep gorge down which flowed a fast-running stream its water boiling white and angry as it raced through the boulders. All around her, other men and women had come to a halt in dismay.

Vera knew that in her present state she would never manage to cross the gorge and the fast-flowing stream. Behind her she could hear the sounds and shouts of the Tommies as they beat the woods, getting ever closer. She must act.

Then she spotted it. Two firs had somehow or other grown together to form a kind of green cradle, which, although fragile, might well support her weight. Ignoring the burning pain in her lacerated legs, she reached upwards and grasped the nearest branch and heaved.

Next moment she had buried herself in the tops of the two trees, hanging on desperately, her heart pumping furiously, watching the last act of the terrible tragedy of von Pannwitz's 15th Cossack Corps.

Now in their terror, the Cossacks began to jump into the water in a last desperate attempt to escape, as the British soldiers burst through the trees. An old, white-bearded man flung himself over the bank. His fragile legs snapped like matchwood and he lay there, slowly drowning, moaning piteously, before his head disappeared under the furious white water. A young woman, naked from the waist downwards, slipped on the bank and plunged screaming into the water. Her companion, a young Cossack soldier, hesitated, as if he were about to rescue her. But before he could do so, a Tommy had struck him over the head with his rifle butt and he pitched to the ground unconscious. Below the woman was torn free from her hold on a boulder and was swept away to her death.

A couple of Tommies, tears streaming down their faces at the sight of the men and women dying in the stream, dropped their rifles and ripping down fir branches, flung them into the water so that the Cossacks might cling to them. A woman, howling like a crazed beast, dodged between them and before anyone could stop her she had raised the child clinging to her breast high into the air and flung it into the abyss!

'Mama, mama,' the other child, clinging to her skirt, cried piteously, 'don't ... *please don't!*'

But the woman's mind had gone. 'I must, I must!' she cried, her lips flecked with froth. Picking up the other child, she flung it too into the water.

'God forgive me!' she screamed. She made the sign of the cross and jumped herself the next moment.

Sobbing hysterically, Vera buried her face into her hands. She could look no more.

Five minutes later, it was all over. Here and there there was still some semblance of military discipline among the British infantry battalion. A handful of the soldiers moved back through the forest, purposefully herding their dejected, sobbing prisoners before them towards the waiting trucks. But the majority no longer cared. They staggered back aimlessly, dragging their rifles behind them, their shoulders bent, their eyes fixed on the ground, as if they could not bear ever to look their fellow human beings in the eyes again.

Their colonel watched them trail past, all military discipline and pride gone, ignoring him and his officers completely, groping their way to the vehicles like blind men. Then he, too, could stand it no longer. 'Come on,' he snapped to his officers, 'the British Army will never do that kind of thing again.'

But the young infantry colonel was wrong. They would.

In her hiding place, Vera Krasnova waited till the sound of the departing trucks and half-tracks had finally died away. Alone and lost, sobbing heartbrokenly and lifting her gaze only to avoid stepping on the dead, she began to walk south into the unknown.

CHAPTER 2

'Impossible, Keightley!' the tall, aristocratic field-marshal snapped angrily, eyes blazing. 'No wonder the Tommies didn't like the job. Who would? I mean, to push thousands of men who didn't want to go across the border into the hands of the Reds, who probably would have butchered them as soon as our chaps were gone.'

General Keightley, the Commander of the Vth Corps, which had moved von Pannwitz's Cossacks across the demarcation line at Judenburg, said nothing. Usually the Supreme Commander Field-Marshal Alexander was the epitome of the cool, collected, urbane Guardee. In all their campaigning together he had never seen Alexander this angry.

'You know, Keightley, some of those officers your chaps delivered to the Reds actually served under me in the Baltic in 1919 when we were fighting the Bolshies up there. A goodly number have British decorations. Why von Pannwitz himself was a company commander in my own Baltic *Landeswehr*! And the British Army delivered gentlemen like that into the Reds' bloody hands!'

Keightley seized the opportunity to intervene. 'I understand your feelings very well, sir,' he said hastily. 'You can imagine what I felt when I heard from the Brigade Commander just how deep morale has slumped after the Judenburg business. But I've got an enormous refugee problem as it is up there in Austria, and simply not enough men to deal with it. I don't like this business any more than you do, sir. But after all, those Cossacks did fight for the Hun — against us indirectly.'

Alexander conquered his rage. His whole conduct had been dominated by the rule that a Guard's officer, especially an Irish Guards' officer, did not display his emotions in public. Ostracism in the mess, or worse, dismissal from the Brigade, might well be the result if he did. When the Supreme Commander spoke again, his voice was calm. 'But my dear Keightley they did not fight against us *directly*, did they!'

'No sir.'

'And that is a point in our favour?

'What do you mean sir?'

Alexander looked at the huge Corps Commander thoughtfully. Keightley was an excellent soldier, but like most of his military subordinates he had no political awareness. He had no idea of what was really happening in the northern Med. He knew nothing of the Russian liaison teams who were everywhere, searching for their nationals in order to repatriate them to their own country. But that wasn't their main purpose in Allied territory; they had other reasons — military and political — for being there. 'Keightley,' he said, 'I'm going to be quite frank with you, but what I'm going to tell you is strictly off the record, as our American friends say?'

'Yessir.'

'Well, it is like this. The Reds' liaison people here in Italy are continually requesting permission not only to visit the POW cages and refugee camps to root out their own people, but they also want to check my Polish troops for their own nationals. Only last week, they put in an application to go to Crete of all places! Now what do you make of that?'

Keightley was a little embarrassed. 'I'm afraid I'm a bit out of my depth, sir. There are no Russian civvies or soldiers who fought for the Hun in Crete, are there, sir?'

'Of course not,' Alexander snapped 'It is just another excuse for people like that terrible toad Colonel Serov to do a bit of spying or slip in some Soviet propaganda.'

'But why, sir?' The Corps Commander could not quite conceal his astonishment. 'I mean the war's over and they are our Allies.'

'Why? Because the Russians are intent on carving themselves a sphere of influence in the Balkans and Southern Europe. Stalin has already got Romania, Bulgaria and Yugoslavia under his control. I mean Tito came straight from Moscow in forty-two to take over the communist partisan movement. So he's obviously their man. Now it's pretty obvious what Stalin's next objectives are?'

'Greece and Italy?' the Corps Commander asked a little hesitantly.

'Right in one, Keightley, especially Italy. Tito's partisans are already making threatening noises at Trieste. He's got a whole division up there in the suburbs, looking as if they are ready to march in and claim the place of the Reds at the first convenient opportunity. Up in the northern part of Italy, the Italian Reds are in complete control, doing virtually what they damn well like. Now imagine a collective operation by Tito and the Italian Red partisans and you might well find yourself isolated in Southern Austria with the whole of Italy north of Milan right up to the Brenner Pass in communist hands.'

'But you can't mean that, sir?' Keightley said in astonishment.

'I certainly can. This summer could well be a very hot one for my command. And the trouble is I simply don't have the men on the ground to ensure that Tito and his Russian pals are dissuaded in time from doing anything stupid. Every day I'm losing thousands of my best chaps to this UK demobilisation scheme and all I'm receiving in return is callow, untrained youths beginning their National Service. As for the Americans,' he shrugged carelessly, 'they simply want to go home.' The field-marshal leaned forward and lowered his voice. 'I need bodies and I might well need them urgently in the near future — men who would be prepared to fight against the Reds if the occasion arose. That business at Judenburg the day before yesterday is going to be the last in my command.'

'I see, sir,' Keightley said, knowing the risk Alexander was taking by such a course of action. Hadn't America and England signed a secret agreement at Yalta the previous February to repatriate all Soviet citizens located in the West once the war had ended? 'And my role in this?'

'In your Corps area you have the Black Cossack Division, commanded by a General Bogdan, don't you?'

'Yessir. Some fifteen thousand strong, according to Intelligence.'

'Fine men and a fine commander.' Alexander chuckled. 'I should know. I fought against him at Lievenhof. Now those are the men I might well need in the near future.'

'But, sir,' Keightley protested. 'I've already briefed my chap Braine of the 133rd Independent Yorkshire Brigade to plan an op against them, if they won't move up to Judenburg peacefully.'

'Well, cancel it!' Alexander snapped.

'But London,' Keightley objected, 'Westminster is pushing the repatriation scheme for all it's worth. What if the Cabinet finds out that you are holding back, sir?'

'A bunch of parlour pinks!' Alexander dismissed the new Labour Government with contempt. 'Let that be my worry. I'm writing to the War Office today to suggest that any Russian in our hands who doesn't want to go back should be classed as stateless immediately. And if that doesn't influence the Foreign Office and their new masters, a calculated leak to the popular press about the sort of thing that's going on at Juden-burg might do the trick.'

The Supreme Commander winked suddenly at a very surprised General Keightley. 'By this time next week, that rogue Bogdan and his Black Cossacks might just well be stateless. Then we'll see what Serov thinks of that!'

CHAPTER 3

The girl reeled down the burning Italian road, staggering as if she were drunk, her bare legs mottled by black caked blood.

Bored a little by the oppressive heat of the day, Bogdan and Boris had ridden out for exercise and sport. Now, their horses reined in, they watched the girl through their binoculars. Since they had captured the village a month before, only a handful of Italian civilians had come their way. Perhaps the word had spread through the local populace what would happen to them if they fell into the Cossacks' hands, especially if they were female, young and pretty.

Bogdan focused his glasses on the girl's face. Her dark brown hair was thrown straight back from a bold, tanned face, dominated by level, deep-blue eyes and a straight, imperious nose.

'She's a succulent Italian pigeon, General,' Boris said with a grin, lowering his glasses and noting the admiring look on the big Cossack's face.

'That she is,' Bogdan agreed, lowering his glasses too. 'But what the hell is she doing in this God-forsaken neck of the woods?'

'Why don't we ride down and find out, General?'

They began the descent of the steep, rocky hillside. As they reached the bottom, the girl saw them. Raising her eyes, she croaked through parched lips:

'*Voda ... pashalsta voda, Gospodin!*'

'Did you hear that, General? She spoke Russian!'

Bogdan slapped the white stallion, 'Come on Boris.' With a flourish he reined in in front of the beautiful girl, who couldn't be a day older than twenty, and asked: '*Gavoritsya vu pa russki?*'

The girl looked up at him in utter disbelief and exhaustion. '*Da, da,*' she croaked through scummed, bloody lips.

'Are you Russian, woman?' he asked excitedly.

The unknown girl drew herself up proudly. 'No, *Gospodin,* not Russian, but *Cossack!*'

Then she fainted.

'But who are you? Where have you come from?' Bogdan asked softly, looking down at the girl, who was stretched out on his bed, with the Divisional Surgeon standing nearby.

'My name is Vera Krasnova,' she whispered weakly, staring at him, dark circles under her eyes. 'My father is — was,' she shrugged a little helplessly. 'I don't know even if he is alive.'

'Tell me his rank, that's all'

'Colonel in von Pannwitz's 15th Cavalry Corps — Cossacks to a man.'

Bogdan knew of von Pannwitz. He was a Baltic German, who had served in the old Imperial Russian Army and had fled to Germany after the failure of the counter-revolution against the Bolsheviks in 1920. In 1942 he had formed a German officered division of Cossacks, which had later been expanded to a corps and had been employed mainly in anti-partisan operations. The last he had heard of them was that they were fighting Tito's partisans in Northern Yugoslavia. They had, he knew, a reputation for brutality, levelling any village suspected of harbouring Tito's men.

'And where is the Corps now?' Bogdan asked.

'What is left of it is in the Drau valley, just below Lienz across the Austrian border to the north of here. A week or so ago, the Corps' Cossack officers decided to break with the

German command. My father and the rest thought we would stand a better chance of surviving if we took our fate into our own hands.'

Bogdan nodded his curly head encouragingly. 'I understand. We did the same. But go on.'

'Well a week ago the first British appeared. In the beginning they were very good. We had lost all we had in the retreat from Yugoslavia and we had little to eat. The British gave us blankets and food.' Her beautiful weary face gleamed with a momentary flash of girlish animation. 'Then when they had been there for a few days, they asked us to surrender our weapons. They said that as we had weapons of so many different countries, German, Austrian, Yugoslavian, Russian and the like, they could not supply us with the correct ammunition. In return we would eventually be given British rifles. We agreed to surrender our weapons to them.

'Stage two of their plan soon followed. They announced they wanted all our officers to attend a conference at Oberdrauburg, which was twenty kilometres away from our positions. Their general wanted to discuss the future of the Cossack Corps with our officers. The plan worried them. Why should 1,500 Cossacks ride twenty kilometres to meet an English General, when it would be much simpler for him to visit them? But in the end the English convinced our officers to go to Oberdrauburg.'

'And?' Bogdan urged her, noting the sudden trembling of her lower lip.

'My father told me not to worry. He would come back. The English were gentlemen who never broke their word. He promised in the name of their King George.' She swallowed hastily. 'That was the last I saw of my father — the last we saw of the whole Cossack officer corps. They never came back.'

'But what happened to them?' Boris asked quickly.

'I don't know. None of us did. But we could guess.'

In short, abrupt phrases, interspersed with sobs, she told the grave-faced Cossack officers what had happened at the camp when the British infantry had come to take them away and of the subsequent bloodbath. 'So you see, General, the English had planned it all along. First the disarmament. Second the separation of the officers. Third the attack on the simple soldiers and their dependents. I began —' She broke off suddenly and buried her face in her scratched bloodstained hands.

Bogdan glanced at the bespectacled Divisional Surgeon. He understood immediately. Taking the girl's arm in his left hand, he pressed home the waiting hypodermic. She cried out, just once, with the sudden pain. A moment later she gave a deep sigh of relief. Her eyelids fluttered and her head fell to one side, as she slipped away into blessed oblivion.

'Well, General?' Boris asked, 'What do you make of that?'

'Boris, to tell you the truth, I don't know.' He tugged at the leather bag of earth around his neck uneasily. 'The Black Cossack Division is different from von Pannwitz's Corps. It was staffed entirely by Fritz officers for one. Two, they had fought against the Western Allies. Thirdly, the Corps contained many émigré officers who had fought against the Reds during the Civil War and were hated by Stalin, Ataman Naumenko, Pyotr Krasnov and the like.'

Boris nodded his understanding.

'Fourthly, von Pannwitz's Corps was officially classed as an SS Corps. We are none of these things, Boris. Perhaps the Tommies will have sympathy with our position.' Boris flashed the General his standard smile, but there was no warmth in his eyes; they were too anxious.

'General, if I can be frank, the only place we will find sympathy is in the dictionary — *and it comes between shit and syphilis!* We are Cossacks and we have fought against Mother Russia. Isn't that enough for Stalin to want to string up each and every one of us?'

'Yes, you're right there. But it doesn't depend upon Stalin, Boris. It depends now on the Tommies — what they will do. And that's something we just can't tell.'

CHAPTER 4

'Well, let's 'ave it, Cadogan,' the burly new British Foreign Secretary ordered, 'what did 'is nibs write?'

Sir Alexander Cadogan, principal adviser to the Foreign Office, the product of Eton and Balliol and nearly forty years in the Diplomatic Service, cleared his throat and began to read out Alexander's message to the War Office in accents which Bevin characterised behind his back as 'cut-glass'.

'A large proportion of these Russians have been repatriated, but there remains a certain number who, because they fear the fate that waits them on arrival in Russia, refuse. To compel them to accept repatriation would certainly involve the use of force.

'Such treatment, coupled with the knowledge that these individuals are being sent to an almost certain death, is quite out of keeping with the principles of democracy and justice as we know them.'

The slim elegant adviser, with the old-fashioned double watch chain dangling across the front of his waistcoat, paused and looked significantly at the most powerful man in the new post-war Labour Government.

'I'll give 'im one thing,' Bevin growled, ''e knows 'is own mind and ain't afraid of saying it. Go on.'

Cadogan cleared his throat and continued. 'Furthermore, it is most unlikely that the British soldier, knowing the fate to which these people are being committed, will be a willing participant in the measures required to compel their departure.

'In view of the circumstances, I recommend that efforts be made to obtain some modification of the Agreement which would allow these people to be treated as stateless persons for the time being. The matter is urgent.'

He stopped reading and holding a copy of Alexander's confidential memo to the War Office between the tips of his manicured thumb and forefinger deposited it carefully on the Foreign Secretary's massive desk. 'That is the sort of thing with which he has been bombarding the War Office, obviously hoping they would take it up with the FO, for the last few weeks.'

'And what does 'e expect we're going to do about it, Cadogan?' Bevin growled.

'Obviously that we rule on the agreement we made with the Russians at Yalta about repatriation, sir. The War Office is sympathetic to Alexander's point of view. Now they expect we should interpret the Yalta Agreement as meaning that force should no longer be used against the Russians, who would under normal circumstances qualify as political refugees, such as those Cossack soldiers I told you about earlier, Minister.'

Bevin considered for a moment, staring thoughtfully at the oil portrait of Palmerston facing him, all Victorian rectitude and power. 'That means 'e's expecting me to 'ave it out with Stalin, ain't 'e?' Bevin said slowly.

Cadogan winced at the battery of dropped 'h's and said: 'Yes, Minister, in essence, that is it.'

'Well it's not on. We're not in a position to 'ave it out with Stalin. As I told the House the other day, Left can talk with Left. With a bit o' luck we can keep him sweet by peaceful means, eh, Cadogan?'

'My sentiments exactly, Minister,' Cadogan answered. 'All these humanitarian considerations on Alexander's part merely cloud the issue. We urgently need peace in the Mediterranean and in order to achieve it, we must come to an arrangement with Stalin. It is vital.'

'Ay,' Bevin agreed. He pointed his forefinger at Palmerston. 'His days are over. We can't go sending a gunboat or two to scare the natives or bang 'em over the 'ead with a big stick. These days the buggers bang yer back!'

'Naturally Minister,' Cadogan answered, preserving the phrase for his upper class friends at the Club — 'These days the buggers bang yer back.'

'For the time being, Cadogan, we'll play this hand straight, cards on the table, faces upwards so that old Uncle Joe don't get any funny ideas. All right what 'ave your boys dreamed up on this one, Cadogan?'

The chief adviser fumbled in his pocket and brought out a single sheet of paper. 'We took the liberty of preparing this for you, Minister.' He tendered it to Bevin, but the Foreign Secretary did not accept the memo.

'Read it to me,' he commanded instead. 'Or better — give me the gist.' He pronounced the word with a hard 'g'.

Cadogan winced at the mispronunciation of the Foreign Office's favourite word. 'Well, in essence, sir, our position is that any proposal to vary the Yalta Agreement might be regarded by the Russians as indicating a general change of our policy towards them.' For the first time since he had entered the Foreign Secretary's office that hot summer morning he allowed himself a faint smile. 'Just in case the gutter press gets on to what is happening out there in Alexander's command and starts kicking up a fuss as they usually do about such things.

'We've thought of this one,' Cadogan continued. 'The FO feels that the British tradition of granting political asylum has always applied to people who reached the United Kingdom or

British territory under their own steam. It does not apply to people who fall into our hands through military operations, such as is the case with these Cossacks.'

Bevin's eyes sparkled suddenly. 'I see what you're getting at Cadogan. You're making out they're not real political refugees.'

'Correct, Minister. We write that it is rather misleading to describe them as political refugees because they have not fled from the Soviet Union, but have been moved westwards by the Germans. It is because of their association with the Boche that they are unwilling to return to their own country. In other words, they are not refugees in the traditional sense. Hence we in the UK will not be breaking our traditional code if we refuse to accept them and send them back to their own homeland.'

'By gum, Cadogan,' Bevin exclaimed in admiration, 'that's the nicest bit of 'air-splitting I've 'eard since I came into the Foreign Office.'

Cadogan cleared his throat importantly. 'I don't know about that, Minister,' he said a little stiffly. 'What counts is the Agreement with the Russians.'

'Right, Cadogan. Bugger the Cossacks.'

Cadogan handed the Foreign Secretary the memorandum. Bevin pulled out one of his battery of fountain pens and scrawled the three words at its foot which one day would constitute a death sentence for the Black Cossacks far away in Italy.

They read: '*Let them go!*'

Field-Marshal Alexander's attempt to save the Black Cossack Division had failed.

CHAPTER 5

Two days later the officers who would carry out the operation against the Black Cossack Division assembled in General Keightley's forward Command Post at Lienz. There was Colonel Serov, his skull freshly shaven and gleaming a little with sweat, his dark eyes excited at the prospect of finally being able to deliver Bogdan to Stalin, but also wary, as they always were when he was dealing with foreigners.

Next to him was Brigadier Braine, known to his troops as 'Birdbrain' on account of his appearance and lack of intelligence. To an obviously contemptuous Serov the man was a caricature of the traditional, hidebound British officer — in short, a fool.

The battalion colonel, who was going to start the planned operation against the Black Cossacks was a different proposition altogether. He was young, bronzed and lean and to judge by the mortar bomb scars which dotted his arms and bare legs like black pepper, he had seen plenty of action in his time. Colonel York's face was bold and determined in a restrained English sort of way. But Serov could see that once Colonel York of the Yorkshire Brigade had made up his mind to do something, he would stick to his decision come what may.

While they waited for Keightley to make his appearance, Serov studied the last of the British officers, Major 'Mad Mike' Evans, York's second in command.

Evans was dark and volatile. In the last twelve months that he had spent as a liaison officer in Italy, Serov had met several such Welsh officers, who looked as if they might well have come from Comrade Stalin's own native Georgia. But it was not Evans' origin which interested Serov; it was his attitude and politics.

Brigadier Braine and Colonel York had welcomed him at Corps HQ politely but with typical English reserve. Major Evans had treated him completely differently. Within five minutes he had involved Serov in an enthusiastic discussion of NEP, the last Five Year Plan, the problems of collectivization in the thirties. Within ten, he had confided in Serov that he was considering leaving the Army and entering politics. 'Naturally just at the moment, one doesn't stand a hope in hell of being elected if one represents the progressive party,' he had told Serov enthusiastically, and the Russian could guess what he meant by that. 'But all the same, the Labour Party is a handy vehicle to carry out the same policies, albeit a little more slowly than in your native country.'

Colonel Serov told himself that the dark, volatile Welshman was his man. He was one of those half-baked intellectual officers he had met in both the American and British Armies, who still believed that they had fought a kind of Popular Front war as in Spain and not an imperialist one, with its objectives the conquest of territory and political and economic gain. Evans, fool as he might be, would be his automatic ally if any trouble cropped up.

'Gentlemen, the Corps Commander,' a soft voice announced at the door.

As one the four waiting officers jumped up from their chairs and sprang to attention as Keightley entered briskly.

He touched his hand to his red banded cap and said, 'please sit down gentlemen.'

Keightley came straight to the point. 'All right, gentlemen, let me put you in the picture. This morning I received a signal from the Supreme Commander's Headquarters. London has ordered Field-Marshal Alexander to clear up that mess in the Karnische Alps and your chaps, Birdie, are the ones who are going to do it.'

Brigadier Braine contented himself with one of his usual 'hms' and a slightly puzzled look appeared on his long face.

'Now let me say this at the outset. I want to avoid a repetition of that nasty business in the Drau Valley if possible. Not only was there trouble with the Russkis, but — excuse me Colonel Serov — the Russian renegades, but there were several cases of indiscipline among our people, especially the junior officers, who didn't like the job.'

'You can — hm — count on my Brigade, General,' Braine said for no apparent reason.

'Of course. I know I can, Birdie. I shall be frank with you all, you too, Colonel Serov. I don't like this business. It is not soldier's work. But if it has to be done — and it has — then it will be done.' For some reason Keightley turned his hard gaze on the young Battalion Commander Colonel York. 'The ultimate decision must lie with the political leaders. After all, one cannot run an army if the soldiers refuse or even question the commander's orders. I hope you *all* understand that?'

Colonel York held his Corps Commander's eye, but by the sudden whitening of his lips, Keightley could see his subordinate was only keeping silent by an effort of will. Next to them, Serov noting the exchange of looks, told himself he'd better keep an eye on Colonel York of the 12th Battalion, the Yorks and Lancs.

Keightley turned towards Braine. 'What I want to say is that this is your op and I don't intend to tell you how to run it. All I want to do is to give you a bit of advice for what it is worth.'

'Fire away, sir,' Braine said cheerfully.

'I feel you must take an oblique approach to the whole business. The Cossacks down there must not learn what is going on until it is too late. You will want to get them in the trains for Judenburg and the Russian Zone before they are aware of what is really happening to them. You understand, Birdie?'

'Hm, yessir,' the Brigadier answered without too much conviction, pondering what the Corps Commander might mean by the 'oblique approach'.

'If I may speak, sir?' It was Colonel York.

'Yes York'

'May I enquire what exactly do you mean by the oblique approach?' the young battalion commander asked, his face serious.

'Well, in the Drau Valley, we first disarmed them under a subterfuge, then we collared their officers by a similar trick, and then we rounded up the rank and file. Unfortunately they cottoned on to what we were about and the result was very messy — very messy indeed.'

York could not conceal his outrage. 'Do you mean the British Army resorted to trickery to get them to come along quietly, sir?'

Keightley looked at him coldly. 'I shall not answer that question, York. And I shall tell you why. Because it is inopportune and impertinent.'

'I am sorry, sir,' York said, tight-lipped and a little flushed, aware that the others were staring at him.

'I accept your apology, York,' Keightley said. 'Now this is what I mean. You, Birdie, and your officers must find a way of keeping the Cossack situation cool until the time comes to get them into the trains for Judenburg. And you must remember they are still armed, unlike von Pannwitz's people.'

'And if they — hm — do resist?' the Brigadier asked, 'or attempt to run away?'

Keightley looked at the shaven-headed Russian Colonel. He knew that every phrase in this room would be relayed to Moscow. Selecting his words carefully, he said: 'If when the time comes to put them in the trains, a person or a body of Cossacks attempt to escape, you will order them to halt by shouting at them. If they deliberately disregard your order and run away, you will open fire aiming at their legs, if you think that this will be enough to stop the attempted escape.'

Keightley paused and took a deep breath. 'If not, shoot to kill! If you are approached by an uncontrollable crowd, you must shoot to kill the apparent leader too. You must not fire overhead or into the air. If you do this the bullet will kill or wound some innocent person. Be quite clear about that, Birdie and ensure that your officers and men are quite clear about it too. If necessary, shoot to kill. *Clear?*'

Evans was enthusiastic about the Corps Commander's determined approach. 'That's the stuff to give them, sir!' he cried. 'They deserve it. After all, they are traitors who fought against their own great country, our ally, Russia.' He uttered the word 'Russia', as if it were in inverted commas.

'Quite so, Major Evans,' Keightley said without enthusiasm, telling himself that this man would be receiving no further promotion as long as he remained in his Corps. Indeed he'd have a word with Field Security about him; the man was obviously a Red sympathiser.

'All right then, gentlemen,' he continued. 'I am going to dismiss you. Colonel Serov here is going to brief you on the background of these Black Cossacks and my staff will fill you in on the details of their present situation in the Karnische Alps. But remember this, I do not want another messy business. Regardless of the way you do it, I want those Russians across the demarcation line without any fuss!'

Colonel York sat alone in the drab little room allotted him at the Corps HQ, slowly getting drunk on the bottle of ration Scotch he had drawn from the Corps Officers' Mess. Outside night was falling and the courtyard below was noisy with the roar of jeeps and motorbikes starting, as officers and men of the HQ set off for Lienz and their Austrian girlfriends. But Colonel York only half heard the roar and the cheerful, bawdy banter of the other ranks below. His mind was too full of the task ahead.

York was a regular officer, who had had 'a good war', as his fellow regulars were wont to call his kind of luck. In six years he had risen from a subaltern to lieutenant-colonel, ending the war as the youngest battalion commander in his division. But he had been glad when the war had ended, glad that he had survived it, glad that the killing had finally stopped, glad that his men could return whole to their families.

But now, when he had thought it was all over, he was confronted with the horror of delivering thousands of men, women and children to another army, which would undoubtedly butcher them in cold blood. Apart from that, the Cossacks were armed. If they realized what the Battalion was about, they'd undoubtedly fight back. That would mean more casualties — two months after the shooting war was over.

He took another drink of the warm whisky and shuddered a little at the taste. Now the brigadier wanted him to take the Battalion up into the mountains and establish first contact with the Cossacks. His job would be to make friends with them until Evans was able to put his part of the plan into operation, which would — hopefully — start them moving northwards to the Ploecken Pass. Once inside Austria they would spring their trap.

Then they would deliver them to the Russians. According to Serov, the officers would be tried by a proper court-martial and if found guilty sentenced to imprisonment. The men would be sent to work on the land and re-educated into becoming 'loyal, useful Soviet citizens' again. But York did not believe one word the Colonel had said.

Had not the whole chain of command from Alex through Keightley, right down to their own divisional commander, General Arbuthnott, protested against the expulsion order! And why? Because they knew what was going to happen to the Cossacks once they had crossed the demarcation line. *They would be massacred!*

And he would be contributing to that massacre. For two whole days, he would have to deceive them, keep them in a fool's paradise, lie, lie and lie again. As the brigadier had commanded, 'Tell 'em anything, York — hm — promise 'em anything — give 'em anything, but don't let the beggars suspect a thing — hm — or we're in the shit.'

Suddenly Colonel York realized that he had become involved in something very terrible. He stared at himself in the cracked mirror on the chest-of-drawers, the room's only other piece of furniture, 'My God,' he said aloud and looked at his drawn face, hardened and prematurely aged by the last six years, 'what the hell am I going to do?'

CHAPTER 6

The Battalion's trucks rolled slowly up the serpentine curves deeper and deeper into the remote mountains. The air was growing cooler and sweeter too. They began to pass through glowing green vineyards and olive groves, through which they could glimpse tumbledown white buildings with russet-tiled roofs. It was a landscape of beauty and peace, in which it seemed all problems should fade and the mind be liberated from care. But he knew that that was an idle hope.

York's scout car swung round yet another bend. Up ahead, a pair of lumbering oxen, urged on by a barefoot, flaxen haired boy armed with a sharp pointed stick, blocked the road. Beyond him lay the first white-painted houses of the village.

'All right, Fred,' York ordered his driver and held up his hand, 'hold it here.'

Fred Deepthorpe from Barnsley, his driver, put his foot on the brake and the scout car came to a halt as did truck after truck behind them.

York cupped his hands around his mouth and bellowed. 'Advance party out now! At the double — there!'

The advance party, sixty strong, jumped from the two leading trucks and formed up under the hard-eyed, ramrod straight, Sergeant-Major Harte of A Company. They were dressed in freshly washed and starched khaki drill, their webbing and rifle slings scrubbed and blancoed. In spite of the heat, the veterans eyed their NCOs with keen alertness, ready to respond to command with uniform precision.

York gave them a quick look of pride. Most of them had served with him since 1939. Then they had been scruffy, bent shouldered immature youths, typical 'street-corner boys' from the North; now they were men, each and every one of them a hardened veteran, who had shed his blood for his country. At that moment he only hoped that they would not end their careers in the British Army being led into some ignoble action.

He dismissed the thought as quickly as it had come. Instead he concentrated on the task in hand. Placing himself at their head, swagger stick clasped tightly at a right-angle under his right arm, he cried: 'Advance party! By the right — *quick march*!'

They were on their way. Behind them, the rest of the Battalion began to spread out among the boulders on both sides of the road, weapons at the ready, just in case…

They marched into the outskirts of the village. Snatches of song reached them from a shady courtyard to their right and York saw powerfully built young men stripped to the waist, washing themselves in buckets, their upper bodies gleaming in the dappled sunlight.

At the sound of marching feet, people streamed out of the houses on both sides. York kept his gaze fixed straight ahead. But he could see the Cossacks, both civilian and soldier, out of the corner of his eye: men in shabby field-grey with black fur caps in spite of the heat; gaunt, dark-skinned women in kerchieves; blond children, sucking their thumbs in awe. But there was no hostility in their faces, just curiosity and perhaps, especially in the faces of the women, a little fear at the sight of these smart, well-armed soldiers who had appeared so suddenly from nowhere. It looked as if he were going to pull it off without trouble after all.

To his left, York caught a glimpse of what looked like the village square, surrounded by larger houses than the rest.

'Advance party — *left wheel*!' he cried loudly, setting a couple of skinny-ribbed dogs barking hysterically.

York's eyes searched the wooden balconies on all sides for the first sign of trouble, as he carried out the drill movement. 'Advance party — will mark time!' he commanded.

The sixty veterans marked time, while the civilians and soldiers gaped at them in undisguised awe. York let them carry out the movement, while he completed his reconnoitre. Nothing!

York clasped his swagger stick more firmly and puffing out his chest, cried: 'Advance party — *halt*!'

As one, sixty right feet crashed down in a cloud of powdery white dust. Suddenly in the echoing silence which followed, York's eye fell on the name of the street in which they found themselves.

Via dei Martiri.

His heart sank suddenly. 'Street of the martyrs!' Was it to be an omen of what was to come?'

For what seemed an age, the two groups eyed one another with curiosity: the immaculate British soldiers, bronzed, tough and lean, most of their arms covered with regimental tattoos; and the Cossacks, uncertain of what might happen. Then suddenly the silence was broken by an old woman who pushed her way through the front rank of young Cossacks, crying in English: 'Don't take us away, Englishmen … don't take us away!'

Caught by surprise, Colonel York involuntarily moved back a pace. But the old woman moved with surprising speed. She thrust her hands up in front of him, crying: 'Look what they will do to us, if you hand us over to them. Look!'

Where her nails should have been, the old woman had scarred flesh. Someone had deliberately ripped out each of her nails!

The old woman saw the look of horror in York's eyes and pressed home her plea. 'Yes, yes, you are right, pulled off with red — hot,' she shrugged wildly. 'I do not know the word in English. But pulled off by those torturers of the NKVD. And they will do worse to us this time, if you English give them our men and women. Believe me.'

York recovered his poise. In his hesitant German, which he guessed many of the Cossacks would understand as well as the local South Tyrolean civilians, he announced at the top of his voice: 'We do not come to harm you. We come as your friends. Now you must regard yourselves as interned until the British High Command decides what is to be done with you. Understand this, we come —' he hesitated for just a fraction of a second, feeling the words stick in his throat, 'as your friends.'

Without waiting to see the reaction to his little speech and sick with self-disgust, he swung round and bellowed at his men in anger: 'Parade — parade, stand at ease! Stand easy!'

The first phase of the great deception had been carried out without trouble. Now everything depended upon the reaction of the legendary General Bogdan.

It was the sound of the trucks and not the marching soldiers which had woken Bogdan from his exhausted sleep in the little bedroom he shared with Vera Krasnova, who had become his mistress exactly twenty-four hours after she had staggered into the village.

Now he stood naked, his body still glazed with the sweat of an afternoon of love-making, at the door to the balcony, watching the square, clumsy looking British three-tonners, packed with infantry, rolling into the village, applauded on all sides by a cheering, clapping happy crowd of Cossacks and civilians, lulled into a sense of security by the British officer's words.

Bogdan pursed his lips thoughtfully and watched the British spring out of their trucks with a professional eye. He could see they were veterans, in their early twenties, the best age for assault infantry. But in spite of their obvious experience, they were taking no defensive precautions. Indeed those of them not engaged in unloading equipment or supplies were chatting happily with his Cossacks in an odd mixture of German and Italian, larded with plenty of sign language and handing out of gifts.

Bogdan began to relax a little. The British seemed to mean them no harm. Surely if this were an offensive operation they would not have entered the village in such a manner, surrounded on all sides by armed Cossacks?

He made up his mind. Tip-toeing softly across the wooden floor, he slipped into his breeches and shirt. He walked to the cupboard and pulled out his black *cherkasske*. He put it on and also his black fur cap. As an afterthought he buckled on his curved silver sabre; but deliberately left behind his revolver. He was ready to meet the British.

'Boris,' he said in a rough undertone as he halted in front of his second in command's room, 'get your evil paws off that girl's tits. The Tommies are here. We'd better make them welcome.'

'At once, General.' There was a sudden squeak of rusty bedsprings, a stifled giggle and then the second in command appeared, tugging on his boots hastily. 'Well,' he said in an unusually low voice for him, 'now we will find out, General.'

Bogdan nodded. He did not need any further explanation of what Boris meant. In the next few minutes their fate would be decided.

They went outside, blinking momentarily in the white light. In front of them the crowd parted, leaving a lane for the two of them to approach the waiting English.

York saw them coming. Serov had briefed him well. The big swaggering fellow in the black coat, criss-crossed with gleaming silver bullet pouches, would be General Bogdan; the other one with the knout and the terrible scarred face would be his chief of staff. Without taking his eyes off them, York barked: 'Advance party — advance party, *attenshun!*'

His veterans carried out the drill movement perfectly. He waited a moment before commanding: 'Advance party — General Officer, present — *present arms!*' In that same moment, as his soldiers' boots slammed down on the ground, York raised his right hand rigidly to his cap.

Bogdan took it all in his stride, as if he were used to receiving such honours from British soldiers, who a moment before he had thought had come to arrest him. He drew himself up to his full height, a head taller than anyone else around him and thrust up his right hand in front of his fur cap in the Russian manner. 'Welcome soldiers!' he cried in Russian, telling himself as he eyed the Britishers that although no one was a better soldier than his own Black Cossacks, these men would be useful soldiers to have on one's side. Then he said in German, 'Thank you, Colonel!'

York stood his men down and accepted Bogdan's handshake, feeling like Judas himself. Slowly he and the enormous Cossack walked the ranks of the soldiers, with Bogdan nodding his head in approval every few seconds. Satisfied, the Cossack faced the British infantry and speaking in slow, hesitant, but understandable German, he said: 'We Cossacks left Russia of our own free will. We joined the German Army, not to protect German interests, but in an attempt to free our homeland. For the last quarter of a century we have had no homeland in Russia. We have been forced from one place to another by the Soviet Government. Our people, men, women and children have been hungry, cold, afraid for twenty-five years. Now we cannot go back.' He looked hard at the young British officer's thin face. 'We ask to be protected by the British Government. But,' he hesitated for only one instant, 'if you wish to return us to Russia, where we will all be surely murdered, then shoot us here and now.'

York could barely speak the few words of reply. 'We come as friends,' was all he could manage, his heart full of self-recrimination.

Bogdan's broad face broke out into a huge smile of relief. He thrust out a hand and took York's. He squeezed it hard and roared. 'Then come, friend. Now we get drunk'

CHAPTER 7

The next twenty-four hours passed swiftly. That very night while he and the shy, almost naïve English Colonel drank large quantities of *grappa*, the British erected a tented camp just outside the Tyrolean village. Unlike the usual haphazard Cossack camp, this was a series of rigid lines of little khaki tents, each separated from the other by a precise distance, according to some formula worked out by their sergeant-major, who (Bogdan noted with amusement) was feared by the soldiers more than they had probably ever feared any German during the war.

He paused at the entrance to the British camp, nodding to the sentries to stand at ease, watching the soldiers with professional interest as they stacked up boxes of rations and supplies at regular intervals among their lines, while others, stripped to the waist in the morning sun and under the command of brisk, determined NCOs, erected a three strand barbed-wire fence around the tented area. To his trained eye, it appeared as if the British were intending to stay at Paulero for some time. It was a good sign.

This impression was reinforced a few moments later when he spotted his groom Mishka standing outside the British kitchen, where soldiers were scouring great steel pans. He talked with animation to a British sergeant, his arms loaded with big ten kilo tins of corned beef.

'What are you doing here, you rogue?' he roared in Russian, as the British sergeant snapped rigidly to attention.

Mishka grinned his toothless smile. 'I am a friend of the English now, General,' he said enthusiastically. 'I admire them.

They are very generous.' He indicated the tins with a nod of his head. 'Look what my friend, Sergeant Smith gave me for that foolish old German Luger. All this real meat, no canned old men like the Fritzes gave us for rations. Now I shall work for the English — with your permission. General? Is true? You my friend, Smith?'

'Sure,' Sergeant Smith answered easily. 'I'm your friend. We're all your friends.'

Bogdan grinned and touched his knout to his fur cap. 'Carry on, Sergeant,' he said in German and then in Russian to Mishka. 'But don't forget your General would prefer something else than the meat of those tired old nags my cook has been serving me these last few weeks.'

'Have no fear, General, this very midday you will taste the succulent, rare Tommy corned beef.'

But if that day, Bogdan grew increasingly more confident that the newly arrived British troops posed no danger to his Cossacks, Vera was of a different opinion. That afternoon after their usual session of love-making in the darkened room, they strolled out of the village to take the air and to be alone. If the beautiful summer's day seemed to symbolize the world's new peace to Bogdan, there was no peace in Vera's heart.

She clung to his brawny right arm, as if he might be dragged away from her forcibly at any moment and her eyes showed signs of fear. Eventually Bogdan stopped at one of the conical haystacks of the area and pushed her down in the grass-scented shade behind it saying: 'Well, come my little dove, spit it out. What is the problem?'

'The English,' she answered immediately.

'What about the English?' he asked carefully, gently stroking her fine young breast.

For a moment she did not answer. All around them the summer heat imposed a vast silence in which the sounds of British and Cossack voices from the village seemed as tiny and as isolated as the drone of the insects in the hay. 'I don't trust them,' she said finally.

He tweaked the nipple of her right breast and felt it respond in spite of her preoccupation. 'I understand. The business with your father and the von Pannwitz Corps.' He shrugged lazily. 'But then the circumstances were different. Von Pannwitz and most of the Fifteenth's senior officers were German. Besides, you saw how friendly that young Tommy Colonel of theirs was last night, Vera?'

Vera's sad, worried expression did not change. 'So was the one they sent to my father's Corps. He had tears — real tears — in his eyes when he was at last forced to tell us what he had done, how he had betrayed us all along, right from the very start. All the same, he *did* betray us.'

'What do you expect me to do, Vera?' he asked softly. 'Even if I did suspect they were going to betray us, what could I do — fight them?'

She shook her head. 'No, we Cossacks can no longer fight back. There are too many of them. They are everywhere now. And there are too few of us. No, Alexei, all we can do is to run.'

'But where to, Vera?' he protested softly. 'How does one organize the escape of a whole Division effectively? We thought they wouldn't find us in this remote valley, but they did.'

'I don't mean the whole Division, Alexei.' She hesitated for only an instant. 'I mean us — you and me. Just the two of us.'

Bogdan reeled back, as if she had slapped him physically, his eyes full of shock. 'But ... but, I couldn't abandon the

Division, Vera! Those men trust me with all their heart. What would they do without me?'

'Alexei, it's our only chance. The only chance perhaps for all of us. To break up now and sneak away in little groups before the Tommies get organized and do the same to us as they did to von Pannwitz's troops.'

'Vera,' he interrupted her. 'There will be no disarming the Black Cossack Division, not until I have a written agreement from the British that they will not send us back to the Soviet Union. Nor will there be any separation of the officers from the men. This Division stays together — and that includes you and me — until our fate in the west is decided.'

'But —'

'There are no buts, my little pigeon.' With his free hand, he pushed her backwards into the hay, spreading her legs with his knee as he did so. She tried to protest, but he stifled her protests gently but firmly. The weight of his massive body descended upon her and suddenly all danger was forgotten in a crazy world of frenzied ecstasy.

On the second day after the British had arrived in the village, Bogdan decided that it was time that the question Vera had indirectly raised should be answered: what was going to happen to him and his men?

Sitting with the young infantry colonel outside his tent that warm summer evening, savouring the fine whisky York had offered him, he posed that overwhelming question.

The Englishman took his time. For a few minutes he made great play of stuffing and lighting his old briar pipe and sipping his drink, his gaze fixed on the ground. Finally he spoke. 'General, I don't think I am in a position to answer that one. After all I am only a simple soldier and not a politician.'

Bogdan frowned. It was not the kind of answer he expected from the young English officer, but he told himself that perhaps the difficulties of talking in German had obscured the point he was trying to make.

'Well,' he tried again, 'let me put it like this, Colonel. What are your orders in respect of my Cossacks?'

Colonel York raised a weak smile, though he had never felt less like smiling in all his life. 'Under normal circumstances, General, that is certainly not a permitted question. But I feel I am not betraying a military secret if I tell you what they are. They are to ensure that order in this part of the world among both the civilian and the military population. In other words, a police job.'

'I see. But how long will your Battalion be needed to maintain that role? The Tyrolean's are peaceful enough and my hot-headed youngsters are quiet, now that they've got those Italian girls to keep them busy in bed at night.' He grinned at the Englishman. 'My officers and a couple of local civilian policemen are all that are needed to keep this area quiet these days. Colonel York.'

'Yes, yes, of course, your Cossacks are exceedingly well disciplined. I wish my own bad lads would learn a little more discipline from them.'

'So?' Bogdan persisted, frowning a little now at the way the Englishman was evading the issue.

'So,' Colonel York echoed a little helplessly, the smoke from his pipe curling up slowly and wreathing his embarrassed face. 'So, soon I shall be forced to take you —'

But Colonel York of the 12th York and Lancs Regiment was not fated to betray his terrible secret to the Cossack General. For at that moment when he knew that he would not lie any more, the well-remembered, high-pitched hiss of a Spandau machine gun broke the silence to the east, and excited voices began shouting everywhere in German, Russian and English: '*The partisans — the partisans are attacking!*' Colonel York's future career in the British Army had been saved and 'Operation Cossack' had begun, right on time.

BOOK THREE: *OPERATION COSSACK*

CHAPTER 1

The heavy partisan machine guns opened up with frightening suddenness. Hammering away like angry woodpeckers they caught the weary Cossacks by complete surprise. Most of them were young enough and quick enough to drop their hay forks and hit the ground. But a couple of older men reacted too slowly. One went down screaming, with what looked like a line of red buttonholes abruptly stitched across his chest. Another pitched silently bn his face, his false teeth flying out with the force of the impact, blood pouring out of his gaping mouth like water.

'Stand by,' an NCO among the Cossack party cried hoarsely. 'Here come the spaghetti bastards!'

Peering over the long yellow grass, the anxious Cossacks could see the dark figures of the ambush party coming slowly towards them, spread out in a long line.

'What are we going to do, Sergeant?' somebody asked in alarm. 'Those macaronis'd cut your gizzard as soon as look at you!'

The Sergeant glanced behind them. About a hundred metres away there was a thick grove of olive trees. He made a quick calculation. In a few moments the partisans would be too close for the machine gunners on both flanks to fire safely without hitting their own men. Then it would be up to the advancing partisans to hit them if they made a break for it.

'All right,' he snapped, with the authority of five years' of war in his voice. 'When I say go, run like hell for those trees — and for Chrissake, don't bunch!'

'What about you, Sergeant?' someone asked.

'Hold yer water, soldier,' the NCO said, drawing his pathetically small Walther, the one weapon the Cossacks possessed. 'I'll look after myself.'

The moments passed leadenly. The black-clad partisans, their upper bodies ringed with bandoliers of ammunition, heavy German stick grenades hanging from their leather belts, came ever closer, wading their way through the grass like beaters at a bird shoot. The Sergeant felt his hand begin to tremble violently, as he raised the pistol and focussed it on the bareheaded man who walked slightly ahead of the rest.

'All right,' he cried, 'get ready.'

Around him, the young Cossacks, their faces suddenly very pale, tensed. 'NOW!' he barked and in the same instant as he fired, they were up and running in crazy zig-zags for the protection of the olive trees.

At the head of the partisans, the bareheaded man flung up his hands in a melodramatic gesture and pitched forward. A second later, the whole line of partisans erupted in wild angry fire.

The NCO, cool and contained now, fired again. Another partisan fell and lay still. They broke into a run, firing from the hip as they came. A stick grenade sailed heavily through the air. It exploded behind the lying man. The NCO shouted with pain, as the red-hot steel shrapnel sliced into his back. But he kept firing. Another partisan clapped his hand to his shoulder and spun round before falling to the ground. And then the line of running men submerged the lone Cossack.

A heavy, nailed boot slammed into his face. He howled with pain. Next instant, a brass rifle butt crashed into the back of his head. He blacked out instantly. Now the partisans could hear the sounds of the hurrying vehicles coming up from the village and the angry alarmed cries of the main body of the Cossacks. They had no time to lose.

'Quick!' their commander ordered.

Two of them, bearded, dirty, ex-factory workers, who had joined the Garibaldi Brigade at the beginning and who had been completely brutalized by two years of the most savage kind of fighting, ripped at the unconscious Cossacks' black breeches. A knife flashed. The unconscious man came to with a scream of absolute, unbearable pain. His spine arched in a taut bow. The partisan with the curved knife slashed his loins again. He screamed again and went limp, his head lolling to one side. An instant later they were running wildly back the way they had come, leaving the horrible mutilated Cossack behind them, his white legs apart, a mess of bloody gore where once his manhood had been.

'By the Holy Virgin of Kazan!' Bogdan breathed in horror and crossed himself hastily, as Boris brushed away the greedy flies which were already beginning to buzz around the wound and revealed it in its full horror. 'To do *that*!' Hastily he stripped off his short jacket and draped it over the body. 'Why? Why now the war is over?'

But he received no answer to his question. Instead the young blond *sotnik*, who spoke Italian, cried from where the couple of fallen partisans lay: 'General — General Bogdan, this one is still breathing!'

Hastily Bogdan, followed by Boris and Colonel York, strode through the dry grass to where the *sotnik* was standing, and peered down at the dark-clad Italian, who lay groaning piteously on his right side.

Mercilessly, Bogdan thudded his heavy jackboot into the Italian's side. 'Wake up!' he commanded harshly in Russian.

York bit back his cry of protest. Such treatment was part of the disgusting lie he had to live at the moment. He would have to keep his peace.

The *sotnik* repeated Bogdan's command in Italian and kicked the dying partisan himself for good measure. The Italian groaned and turned round.

York gasped. The dead Cossack NCO's bullet had caught him squarely in the right side of his face. It was a bubbling mess, looking as if it had been chewed away by some wild animal. The typical wound of a dum-dum bullet.

'Make him open his eyes,' Bogdan commanded.

The *sotnik's* steel-shod boot thudded into the dying man's ribs, splintering them audibly. 'Eyes — open your eyes!' he yelled.

The Italian's dark eyes, liquid with pain, flickered open to stare uncomprehendingly at the circle of harsh, angry foreign faces looking down at him on the ground. '*Una sigar-etta … sigaretta, per favore,*' he gasped. 'I die.'

'*Cigarette!*' Bogdan cried, understanding that much Italian and beside himself with rage. 'If I had one, I'd burn your goddam treacherous Italian eyes out with it! *Sotnik,* ask him why they attacked us now. *Quick!*'

The dying partisan closed his eyes and said nothing. Bogdan carried away by rage, grabbed the man's long black hair and pulled him up by it cruelly. 'I asked you a question, you bastard!' Freeing one hand he slapped the partisan savagely across the face. His knuckles were suddenly flushed with blood. With the last of his strength, the dying man hawked and spat directly into Bogdan's face.

'*That's why,*' he gasped, as Bogdan, pale with shock, the spittle dripping down the side of his face, let go of his hold and the partisan dropped back to the ground.

Crazily in a wild cracked voice, the dying partisan sang the *Bandiera Rossa*, as the grim faced Cossacks bound him to the olive tree with his own belt and those of his fallen comrades. Swiftly they stepped back as the *sotnik* in charge of the impromptu firing squad of shirt-sleeved Cossacks, armed with a hastily grabbed assortment of weapons, stood the men to attention.

York breathed out hard. He knew he was watching an illegal action. The Cossacks were prisoners of war, ex-enemy soldiers. They were not allowed to shoot the British Army's 'co-belligerents,' as the Italian troops were officially called at Headquarters. It was his duty to step between the firing squad and the man, tied to the tree, singing in a crazy, toneless voice. Yet he knew he must not. He must not explain; he must not protest. He must sustain the friendship of these wild angry cavalrymen until the trap was sprung and the whole miserable, disgusting business was over.

'Take aim!' the *sotnik* cried.

'Fire!'

The *Bandiera Rossa* came to an abrupt end. As the sharp crack of musketry echoed and re-echoed among the surrounding heights, the partisan's head sank to one side. Briskly the *sotnik*, pistol already in hand, marched towards the Italian. He didn't bother to check whether the man was breathing still or not. Instead he placed the muzzle of his pistol to the back of his head and pulled the trigger without hesitation. The Italian's skull smashed and disappeared in a welter of blood.

For a moment, Bogdan stared at the limp figure of the dead man hanging by the belts at the tree, then he swung round to face York, his face set in harsh resolution. 'I should like to speak to you about this business, Colonel.'

York forced himself to answer by a sheer effort of will. 'Yes,' he said thickly. 'I think we'd better discuss it, General'

The Cossack Leader had fallen for the bait!

CHAPTER 2

Colonel Serov lowered his glasses slowly and gave Major Evans, crouched beside him behind the boulder, his cold-eyed smile.

Evans smiled back with his usual unthinking enthusiasm and raised his thumb in the sign of victory. On both sides of them, the Partisans of the Garabaldi Brigade streamed back to their mountain village HQ, where the feast and the girls Serov had promised them would be waiting. Evans waved heartily at their leader. The partisan looked enquiringly at Serov. The Russian nodded slightly and the partisan flashed a brief smile at Evans. A few moments later they were gone, leaving the two officers alone.

'Well,' Evans broke the heavy silence that had descended upon the mountain slope. 'It looks as if it worked.'

Serov did not answer. He did not need to pander to the Englishman's foolishness. Evans did not notice. 'Well, we've done our bit, Colonel,' he prattled on. 'Pity about the — er — comrades, getting hit like that at this stage of the game. But they died for the cause.'

Colonel Serov restrained his sneer of contempt just in time. Evans was his strongest ally in the British camp; he must keep him sweet. 'Yes, but not in vain, Major Evans. Now it will be up to Colonel York to do the rest, to get them moving.'

'Old Yorkie! He's a bit of a stickler, old-fashioned, and all that. But he can be very persuasive when necessary. I remember once just before Alamein when the Battalion —'

'Quite, quite,' Serov cut him short with barely restrained impatience. In these last months with the Anglo-Americans, the very mention of that battle in the remote desert made him see red. How they prated about it, a battle which was just a skirmish when compared with Stalingrad! 'I am sure he is. Your York will convince them. They'll move. The question is, will that traitor Bogdan fall for the second stage of our plan?'

Evans responded immediately. 'Oh, I think so, sir. Our people at the border have got it all laid on. Very well planned. Even old Birdbrain, hm — the Brigadier can't make a balls-up on this one, even if he tried. It's in the bag.'

'It'd better be, Major. Comrade Stalin would be very angry if the Cossack traitor escaped his just fate. Now then,' his voice grew a fraction less harsh and he smiled winningly at the other man, 'I trust you, Major, more than the others.'

'Oh, they're all right, Colonel. Just a bit reactionary that's all. Typical Army — Regular Army, I mean,' Evans said easily.

'Just so. All the same, Major Evans, I would like you down there in the Cossack camp, just to ensure that everything goes to plan.'

Evans frowned a little. 'Really, the Colonel said I was to stick with you, sir. As liaison.'

'I know, I know. But I think you'd serve a better purpose down there making sure everything runs smoothly. After all, it is better to have one of our own kind there. Yourself, eh? *Horosho, tovarisch?*'

Evans beamed hugely at being addressed as a 'comrade.' '*Horosho, tovarisch,*' he said happily, and rose to return to his jeep. Five minutes later he was rolling merrily along the mountain trail in the direction of the village.

Scrov watched him disappear round the bend in a cloud of white dust; then he spat contemptuously on the parched ground.

For 'Mad Mike' Evans the outbreak of war had been a heaven sent opportunity to avoid making a decision about what he should do after his Cambridge career. The Army had solved that particular problem for him.

Evans took to the life like a duck to water. His burly body and vigorous, if simple mind responded immediately to this new existence. He was actually allowed, indeed encouraged, to drive his own body and those of the men under his command to the limits of physical endurance. Here was a sport — that of killing on the battlefield — which was more exhilarating, more exacting, more dangerous than anything he had known hitherto.

Within six months of being posted to his battalion after receiving his commission, he was already nicknamed 'Mad Mike' by his own men. For of all the officers in the battalion they knew the hearty, ever enthusiastic Welshman was the most likely one to 'land them in the shit' when the time came for them to go into action.

On the battlefield he proved them right. He was careless of his men's lives, eager for adventure and glory. Evans, however, revelled in the danger, always ready to volunteer his own platoon — and later company — for the most dangerous missions. And woe betide any German prisoner who fell into his hands! If there were no senior officer present, the unfortunate 'Jerry' was not likely to live long. As he told his men often: 'In my company we don't take prisoners! They only gum up the works!'

Until Sicily Evans had had a splendid war. But during the fighting around Mount Etna in 1943 he was wounded and left behind by the battalion when they crossed over into Italy. He hated the base hospital. Everywhere the administrators had moved in after the fighting troops had moved out: middle-aged base wallahs with no conception of war as he knew it.

For a while, he considered reverting to orthodox religion to alleviate his depression but the little Sicilian nurse whom he seduced on the night shift during her first week at the British military hospital had taught him a different type of religion. Marxism!

Suddenly 'Mad Mike' Evans became aware of a new current in the affairs of man which would lead to a braver and better world: the cause of world revolution. Afterwards when he had returned to the battalion (and the little nurse had found that her Sicilian 'comrades' were as bourgeois as the older generation had ever been about a single girl with an increasingly large belly, he had tried to spread the word in the occasional 'ABCA' lecture and 'current affairs' talk in their periods out of the line. But the veterans had not been interested. Their sole concern had been survival, the next hot meal, a bed, and a bit of the other! The cause of world revolution left them cold.

Major Evans was undismayed. He told himself that the men had been conditioned too long by service in the Army, a reactionary, class-conscious organization, which had killed all awareness that these one-time workers might ever have had of the 'class struggle.' Instead, as the war slowly began to creep towards its end, he started to prepare himself for his new career in politics.

This then was Major 'Mad Mike' Evans, MC and bar, at the age of 26, who thirty years later would figure as an exceedingly cynical, corrupt and prominent member of the government front bench. Major Evans now sped towards the Cossacks' camp in his open jeep to institute his first attempt at political betrayal: a course of action for which he was to become justifiably notorious in the House of Commons in the years to come. His political career was about to begin!

CHAPTER 3

Bogdan downed the whisky in one gulp and looked angrily at a silent but determined York. 'Why?' he demanded in German. 'Why now?'

The British Colonel wiped the thin film of sweat from his brow. 'Because they hate you and your people, General, I suppose,' he replied.

'But the war's over. What happened then was due to the war. Now it's over.'

York shrugged. 'Of course. But the Italians have long memories. They don't forgive easily. Perhaps they've been waiting for an opportunity like this for weeks, waiting till your guard was down, knowing that sooner or later you'd be unprepared.' Colonel York lied glibly. The heat and the whisky helped. Now all he wanted was to get it over and never to see General Bogdan and his Cossacks again. 'Perhaps you're a permanent thorn in their sides. Most of them are communist and here are fifteen thousand Russians who have actively fought against their cause. For them it is almost as if Jesus had — decided to join the Devil in his fight against God. You understand, General?'

Bogdan nodded and looked gloomily at his empty tin mug. Hastily York poured him another generous slug of the precious scotch. He wouldn't sleep this night if he didn't take in at least half a bottle. But it didn't matter. Tonight he must convince the big Cossack officer.

'What do you think, Colonel?' Bogdan asked after taking another drink. 'Do you feel they'll attack again?'

York nodded. 'Of course. You saw what they did to that Cossack of yours. You experienced the full power of their hatred. They'll come again — and there's nothing we can do about it, apart from using armed force. Rome is powerless up here. The partisans are their own government. They do as they please.'

Angrily Bogdan put down his mug on the little rickety table. 'Then by God, my Cossacks will fight back. We shall see who gives in first — the macaronis or us.'

It is not a question of who is the better fighting man, General,' York said urgently, hastily grasping the line the Cossack had unwittingly thrown him. 'Your Cossacks are undoubtedly superior. But that is not important.'

'What is important then, Englishman?' Bogdan growled.

'I'll try to explain, General. You see, the whole political balance in this area is very delicate.'

'Tito you mean?'

'Yes. He has his partisan army poised on the Yugoslavian frontier with Italy, and behind him the Red Army. Both of them, according to our Intelligence, are thirsting for more territory. Soviet imperialism!'

Bogdan gave the Englishman a shadow of a grin. *'Russian,'* he corrected him. 'For nearly three centuries, we Cossacks extended the Czar's territories to east, south and west. Russian imperialism, you are talking about.'

'All right, whatever you say, General. The main thing is that my people don't want to give Tito and his Red pals any excuse for marching into this area.'

'And you think that trouble between my Cossacks and the partisans might be that excuse?'

'Exactly. Renegade Russians, who once fought the Germans, now fighting their communist brothers in Italy with the tolerance and, in the case of this evening, the active assistance of the British.' York paused to let his words sink in completely. 'You can see the problem?'

'I can. The partisans will attack again. If we Cossacks don't defend ourselves, you British will be forced to defend us. But either way Tito and his Russian masters could well use the occasion to march into Northern Italy to assist their Red brothers.'

'Precisely!'

Bogdan considered. There was no sound save the soft tread of the British sentries guarding the camp, the persistent buzz of the moths and the hiss of the petrol lantern on the packing case table. Finally he said: 'You have an idea what can be done about it, Colonel?'

York caught himself just in time. He must not appear to be too eager with his proposal. The Cossack was no fool, in spite of his exotic appearance. He had been betrayed twice before — by Stalin and then by the Germans. Bogdan was wary. 'When I returned to camp after the incident, General, I sent a signal to my superior officer, Brigadier Braine, requesting advice and instructions. In his turn, my Brigadier must have spoken with the Corps Commander Keightley at Lienz. Their answering signal arrived just before we came in here.' He pulled out a brown coloured piece of paper from the tunic pocket of his sweat-stained shirt and put it on the table.

Bogdan did not pick up the signal 'I do not read English,' he said, 'What does it say?'

'The Corps Commander has suggested — in the best interests of all — that you and your Cossacks leave Italy —'

Bogdan's head shot up from the mug of whisky, his eyes suddenly hard and alert. 'Leave Italy, *leave it for where*?'

'Austria.' Hastily York took a sip of whisky to hide the look on his face: he had done it. Now it was out in the open at last!

'Where in Austria?' Bogdan demanded.

'Just over the Ploecken Pass is the Corps Commander's suggestion. There are apparently a couple of villages on the other side, Mauthen and Koetschach, which could house your people decently for the winter. The villages are only a day's march from here too.'

Bogdan noticed the word 'winter'. 'You mean the British would put us up there and support us throughout the winter?' he asked eagerly.

Now York had him! Obviously he had been worried about how he could support his Cossacks throughout the winter on the limited amount of food available at Paulero. 'Yes, General, the British Army would probably be only too glad to feed your people up there in Austria. You would be carefully tucked away in those remote villages and safely out of Northern Italy. The Communists would have no excuse for any sort of political adventures here.'

'You know perhaps what happened to the von Pannwitz Cossack Cavalry Corps in Austria, Colonel?' Bogdan asked suddenly, catching York completely off his guard, for a moment.

'Yes General,' he stuttered. 'I've heard about it.'

Bogdan leaned forward across the table, his bold face hollowed out to a death's head in the glaring white light of the lantern. 'How do I know that the same thing won't happen to the Black Cossack Division? That you British won't send us back to the Reds. He pushed home his argument. 'Have I your word as a British officer, Colonel York, that this time the British will try no trickery?'

It was the worst moment in all of the young Colonel's life. In the past years of war, he had been forced to take many terrible decisions. Every day in the line, an infantry officer has to make decisions which will mean death for men he has served with for years. But never before had he been forced to make a decision of such magnitude as this: a simple lie, which might well cost the lives of 15,000 men, women and children.

'Well?' Bogdan demanded impatiently.

York coughed, and then, as if he were outside his own body, observing himself from under the roof of the little tent, he heard himself saying, 'General Bogdan you have my word as a British officer that we will try no trickery.'

Impulsively Bogdan thrust out his hand and took York's limp hand in his own. He squeezed it hard in a rare outburst of emotion. 'Thank you, Colonel,' he said. 'Thank you from the heart!'

York replied numbly, 'What will you do General? Will you accept the Corps Commander's offer?'

Bogdan rose to his feet, his eyes searching York's face, as though he were looking for something very important there; then he said: 'Colonel York, I shall tell my decision tomorrow morning. Dosvedanya!'

Five minutes later, Major Evans, unshaven, his swarthy face almost black now from a day in the sun, burst through the tent flap. He looked at York crouched over the half empty bottle of whisky, his thin shoulders bent in defeat

'Well, we pulled it off, Colonel,' he bellowed. 'Didn't we? Worked like a ruddy charm. You should have seen the look on the renegades' ugly mugs when the Eyeties hit them on that road...' His words died away in the oppressive silence. 'I say, sir, is there anything wrong?'

'*Oh for Chrissake, Evans, will you fuck off!*'

CHAPTER 4

'Six o'clock, sir.'

York arched his body pleasurably under the khaki blanket. He relaxed and savoured the cool fresh air of the new day, listening to the village and the camp waking up: the clatter of the cooks' dixies; the hoarse dry coughing of some soldier trying his first *Woodbine* of the day; the stamp of the orderly sergeant's boots as he marched from tent to tent, whacking the canvas sides with his cane to wake the occupants.

Every morning of his military life York had enjoyed these first few lazy moments — beautiful and tranquil — before the business of the day began. He woke completely and then he remembered. *This was the day he moved the Cossacks north!* Abruptly he felt sick and defeated.

'Come on now, my lucky lads, let's be having yer!' Sergeant-Major Harte's voice rose as he strode imperiously between the tents, all starched khaki drill and brilliantly gleaming ammunition boots. 'Get on parade!'

Colonel York stared at the grinning men rushing past him to form up, flinging him a hasty salute, wondering why the CO was about at this time of the morning, glad to be on the move again, regardless of where they were going. Again he was seized by that sick, defeated feeling. *This was the day he moved the Cossacks north!* Hastily he shrugged it off, and allowed pride in his Battalion to return, as the companies formed up, one by one, as the feet shuffling confused mass of excited khaki became straight, immaculate, motionless lines.

Consciously York allowed himself to be absorbed into the single organism of his Battalion, in which all individuality and worry vanished: an organism which was self-sufficient, independent, a law unto itself. 'Men,' he cried, raising his voice so that the whole 800 strong Battalion could hear. 'You know what we've to do this day … I want you to do it without complaint. I don't like it, my officers don't, and I know you don't. But it's got to be done. And the 12th Battalion, the Yorks and Lancs will do it.' He let the words sink in. 'All right, Sergeant-Major,' he ended, 'dismiss the Battalion for breakfast!'

The khaki machine had been set in motion!

Seven o'clock, Thursday, 30 June, 1945. The sun had risen. Already the atmosphere was saturated with heat. Bogdan's Cossacks and their women were already preparing to move out, watering their horses; cradling their hands around mugs of syrupy tea, sweetened with honey in the Cossack fashion; smoking their first pipes of the day, lashing the looted tarpaulins over their homemade carts. Within the hour, the start-time prescribed by the English, they would be ready.

Bogdan turned and looked at Vera. She still slept, slack and warm like a sated animal after a night of wild lovemaking, the only sign of life the slow rise and fall of her naked breasts.

'No!' she had cried with a fervour born of terror, when he had told her of his decision. '*No, no, no!*' her fingers had dug painfully deep into the muscle of his right arm. 'Don't trust them, Alexei!'

Gently he had released himself from her grip and said: 'It is the only way, my little dove.'

'They will betray you, just as they betrayed us in the Drau Valley.'

Her impassioned plea had not changed his decision. Half an hour later he had met the English colonel in the square. *Via dei Martiri*, the blue and white sign above his head had read. It had meant nothing to Bogdan.

'Well?' the Englishman had asked almost casually. 'What do you intend to do, General?'

'We march.'

'Good,' the Englishman had replied, his face devoid of any emotion.

'When?'

'Thursday.'

They had exchanged salutes and gone their separate ways. It had been as simple as that. Now the future of the Black Cossack Division lay in the hands of the young English colonel.

Eight o'clock. The animation of the previous hour had vanished now. The Cossack women were nervous, but silent, while their children, impatient to be on their way, were fretful and irritable. The Cossacks for their part were suddenly oppressed, whether due to the growing heat or sudden foreboding, Bogdan did not know.

The General experienced a mood between depression and apathy. In a way he hated to leave the little mountain village. He had been happy here, and, for some indefinable reason, the future disturbed him. Suddenly he felt wretched, stirred from time to time by waves of resentment at the tardiness of the English and the sullen look on Vera's beautiful young face, as she stood at his side.

'Damn the Tommies!' he cursed suddenly so that Boris, to his right, jumped a little. 'When in three devils' name are they going to come?'

'They'll come soon enough, General,' Boris answered gloomily. 'Soon enough. Never fear.'

Bogdan looked at him. 'And what is that supposed to mean, Boris?' he snarled.

'Nothing, General Just a figure of speech.' But the look on his mutilated face told Bogdan that he was lying. Boris was worried, distinctly worried.

Nine o'clock.

The British infantrymen leaned phlegmatically on their rifles, occasionally wiping the beads of sweat from their dripping faces with khaki handkerchiefs, staring at the waiting Cossacks with sullen indifference. The Cossacks, the men already mounted, the women, children and old men in the carts, waited in silence.

A new sound intruded into the dull vacuum of the *Via dei Martiri*: the noise of motors grinding along in first gear. The trucks were coming. The platoon sergeants wiped the sweat off their faces for the last time and turned to face their men. Across the road, the Cossacks started to turn their heads in the direction of the noise. Bogdan's groom, Mishka, relaxed his hold on Don's bridle and waved at Sergeant Smith, in charge of a platoon of armed cooks. Uneasily Smith waved back. Mishka's mouth formed the one word of English he now knew, *'friend.'* Suddenly Smith looked away, as if embarrassed.

Next moment Colonel York's little scout car swung round the corner, followed by the first of the trucks. Bogdan's torpor vanished immediately. His attention was rivetted by the soldier standing upright in the cab of the truck, his upper body poked through the hole in the roof next to the driver, his hands clutching one of the British light machine guns, the Bren. As the next truck came round the corner, Bogdan, suddenly alarmed, saw that it too bore an armed man. The third also. In fact each vehicle in the convoy carried a soldier, armed either with a machine gun or machine pistol, standing alertly next to the driver.

Bogdan exchanged a swift salute with Colonel York, who had sprung lightly from the scout car, and asked without ceremony: 'Why the armed men, Colonel?' His voice was harsh and commanding.

York was prepared for the question. 'The partisans, General. They'll obviously know about this move, and who knows what they might do before we reach the Austrian frontier. I thought it better to have an armed man on each truck.'

'My Cossacks can take care of themselves.'

'I know that, sir. But we want no more incidents. I'm going to ask you —'

'Not to surrender our weapons, I hope?' Bogdan interrupted hastily, seeing the sudden look of apprehension in Vera's eyes.

'Of course not, sir. If we are attacked by the partisans on the road, I'd prefer that my men deal with the matter. If they want trouble, they'll get it from us so that afterwards there can be no complaints that we, the British, are allowing armed POWs or internees to fire on Allied civilians.'

'I see,' Bogdan said, accepting the glib explanation unthinkingly. 'Then that's all right. Now when do we move — and how?'

'My men will get on the trucks now, sir,' York answered. 'My plan is to put one truck between every three of your carts and between each of your squadrons.'

'Won't that make for confusion, Colonel — and for slowness?'

'Yes sir,' York said promptly, his answer already rehearsed. 'It will — and it won't do the engines of my Bedfords much good, running in first gear all day. But I want British soldiers clearly visible throughout the trek. That way I'm hoping to deter a partisan attack.'

Again Bogdan swallowed the explanation. 'A good idea, Colonel.' He smiled suddenly. 'But I never thought I'd live to see the day when the Black Cossacks would need anyone else to guard them.'

York laughed and cupping his hands around his mouth yelled 'All right, you men — mount up now!'

Everywhere NCOs and junior officers started to bawl out orders. The men broke ranks and began to climb into the trucks. In an instant all was controlled confusion and York was glad to submerge himself in the busy routine of the departure.

Bogdan urged his big white stallion through the throng to the head of the leading squadron of Cossacks. Behind him Vera slotted herself into the ranks of the troopers, as much at home on horseback as were the young fighting Cossacks.

Bogdan took one last lingering look at the little Italian village, then he raised his big hand, grateful for the old instinctive routine, 'Cossacks — Cossacks of the Black Division - *advance*!'

His gaze set firmly on the mountains ahead, General Alexei Bogdan started to canter forward. Behind him the Black Cossacks began to advance, six abreast, the rigid riders rising and falling rhythmically and proudly on their immaculately groomed mounts, soldiers once more. The Black Cossack Division had begun its last march.

CHAPTER 5

The long convoy toiled higher and higher into the mountains, heading for the pass. The still air was heavy with the smell of human and animal sweat, and the aroma of the Cossacks' saddles. There was little noise, save the steady clop of the horses' hooves, the creak of the cartwheels and the throaty grumble of the trucks' engines.

Between the cavalry and the carts, the boys and the young girls, their naked feet baked in tar prior to the trek to harden them, drove the Cossacks' looted animals in front of them: heavy russet oxen, flocks of bleating goats, bells jingling merrily at their necks; angry, protesting geese.

The hours passed with leaden feet. Midday came. York ordered a halt. Gratefully the infantry pulled out their tommy cookers and started to brew up at the roadside, watched by the curious Cossack children. The Cossacks, however, parched and exhausted from the long ride in the burning heat, contented themselves with a bucket of water, shared between them and their mounts, before flinging themselves down in whatever shade they could find to sleep.

Major Evans, energetic as ever, dropped behind the boulder where Colonel York was moodily sipping a mug of tea. 'This is the life, Colonel,' he said enthusiastically. 'Fresh air and the mountains, again. Good to get away from that village, isn't it?'

'Is it?' York said without enthusiasm.

'Something wrong, sir?' Evans inquired.

'Of course, there's something wrong, Evans. Everything's bloody wrong! It's wrong what we've got to do. It's wrong that it's this Battalion that has got to do it. It's wrong that I've got to order them to — Oh, Christ!' He took a furious gulp of his tea.

'Do you mind if I say you're getting hot under the collar about this thing, sir. It's just a routine sort of an op. after all. Escort to a bunch of half-baked POWs.'

York turned slowly and looked at the Major, as if he were seeing him for the first time, although they had served together for nearly six years. 'Do you really believe that, Evans?' he asked, his voice low and controlled, yet with an awesome note in it.

'Of course, sir. What else could you call it?'

York shook his head in disbelief. 'I'll tell you what I'd call it, Evans,' he hissed through gritted teeth. 'That is if I had the guts to do so — *I'd call it downright, unmitigated bloody treachery*, that's what I'd call it!'

Evans looked at York, as if he had suddenly gone out of his mind.

Vera Krasnova took her eyes off the two English officers, wondering why the colonel had suddenly become so angry with the other. She turned her attention to Bogdan, snoring softly at her side in the shade of the stunted tree.

In the few short weeks they had been together, the General had become her whole life. Every nerve of her young beautiful body was awake to him. When he frowned, Vera felt she could die. When he spoke harshly to her in his rough Cossack fashion, she did die — for a second.

Yet, in spite of her hero-worship of this man, she knew at this moment he had made a terribly wrong decision. He *was* walking into a trap. The English would betray him. She knew it in her very bones.

But she could not convince Bogdan of that. She knew that she did not live inside him, as he did inside her. Twice before when she had told him of her doubts, he had laughed at her — not scornfully — but he had laughed. And naturally she had no physical evidence with which to convince him. Yet all the same, she could not ignore a kind of physical uneasiness, the little warning signals, such as the fact that the English soldiers were becoming increasingly snappy with the Cossack children the closer the trek got to the Austrian frontier.

As Bogdan slept on, oblivious to the flies buzzing about him in the midday heat, Vera Krasnova stared at the far-away snowy peaks which marked the frontier, knowing that if the trouble did start, it would start up there.

Squatting well away from the boiling dixies of canned 'M and V' stew, Sergeant Smith smoking at the side of his pal Fred Deepthorpe, watched by an admiring Mishka, muttered: 'Poor bastards. Wonder where the poor sods'll be this time next week, eh?'

'In Brown's Garden, pushing up daisies, Smithie,' his pal answered moodily, 'if all I've heard from the lads is true.'

'Ay, happen yer right there, Fred,' Sergeant Smith said wearily and flipped away his *Woodbine*, which was caught neatly by a waiting Mishka before it hit the ground.

'Friend,' he exclaimed gratefully, taking a deep drag. 'Tommy friend.'

'Ay, Tommy bloody good friend all right,' Smith said scornfully, as Major Evans gave a long blast on his whistle to signal the resumption of the trek north. 'Bugger that for a tale!'

They came to the frontier, as the blood-red ball of the sun finally began to sink behind the peaks of the Alps and the sweat started to dry on their tired, dusty faces.

Colonel York was in the lead now. Behind him at fifty yards' distance came the first squadron of Cossack cavalry under Bogdan's command, their mounts hanging their heads in exhaustion after the long climb. 'Slow down,' York ordered, as they swung round a bend in the road and the bullet-pocked, pre-war sign announced in German '*Deutsche Reichsgrenze — 200 Meter.*'

Obediently the driver crashed the gear home and changed down to first. Slowly the scout car began to approach the red and white striped pole which barred the route, the Union Jack flying on one side of it and the red and white eagle of the new Austria on the other.

A shabby Italian frontier guard in a faded light-green uniform came out from behind a boulder, machine pistol held in his dirty hands, his face anxious. But as soon as he saw the British uniforms, the look of anxiety was replaced by a happy smile. 'Okay, boys,' he said loudly, and then squeezing the fingers of his free hand together, he pressed them to his open mouth in the Italian gesture of hunger and cried: '*Fame … fame, signore.*'

Almost without thinking, Colonel York bent down inside the scout car and pulled out a tin of bully beef and flung it to him.

The frontier guard grinned mightily at the Colonel. 'Bloody Italians,' the driver growled, as he began to apply the brakes before the striped pole. 'Always crying stinking fish. Be glad when we're up with the Germans. They've got some sodding pride at least.'

'Just keep your mind on the road, Fred. I'd hate to be writing, a "Dear Mrs Deepthorpe" letter at this stage of the game, you know.'

'I'm watching it, sir,' the driver answered with a grin, halting the scout car neatly five yards away from the lone British sentry, who was accompanied by an elderly Austrian policeman armed with a wooden club.

'All right, soldier,' York said, acknowledging the salute. 'You can open the barrier now and let us pass.'

'You the Cossack convoy, sir?' the sentry asked.

'Yes, we are,' York answered, going through the routine which they had agreed upon with the Brigadier and Field Security beforehand. 'What of it?'

'Begging your pardon sir,' the sentry said humbly, though there was nothing humble about his dark, sharp eyes under the big khaki beret. 'But I wonder if you could pop up the road to see my officer? There's some hitch about letting you through.'

'Why?' York asked, hating himself for going through with this charade.

'Search me, sir. I've only got me orders.'

'All right.' York turned to get into the Dingo.

'And sir.' It was the sentry again. 'My officer said the Cossack gentlemen — their commanders — should pop up and see him too for a couple of minutes.'

'I see.'

York stared at Bogdan and his second in command Boris who were watching the scene silently from fifty yards away, their faces expressing nothing but weariness after the hard day's ride in the blazing heat. He cupped his hands around his mouth and cried in German. 'They want us to wait here for a few moments, General. And the border people would like to speak to me — and you, too.'

Boris glanced at Bogdan, his weariness replaced by suspicion. 'What could the border guards want with you, General?' he demanded. 'Why shouldn't the British take care of that themselves? They are escorting us and they are guarding the border. Let them sort it out among themselves.'

'Don't be a suspicious old woman, Boris. Perhaps the Tommies want to know the Black Cossacks' exact ration strength so that they can feed us. Perhaps it's something to do with the Austrian authorities.'

'General,' Boris said firmly, 'I'm coming with you.'

'As you wish,' Bogdan answered easily. 'I'm sure you're only after some of that good whisky of theirs, which they will undoubtedly serve in my honour there,' He tugged at Don's bit. 'Come on, let's go and see what the Tommies want.'

Behind them, far down the waiting ranks of the first Cossack squadron, Vera watched and stifled a cry of anguish and fear.

The little frontier post, with the legend '*Zollabfertigung*' painted in fading white letters on its bullet-pocked wall, was deserted save for a dusty 15cwt truck outside the door. Instinctively Boris and Bogdan scanned the surrounding area up to the thick grove of firs some hundred metres away. But there was no one. The whole area around the post seemed empty too.

The driver braked, and the armoured scout car came to a halt next to the truck, the rear flaps of which were carefully lashed down. York dropped over the side and waited till the two Cossack horsemen cantered up to where he stood.

'Why do they want us, Colonel?' Bogdan queried.

York squinted up at him in the slanting rays of the setting sun. 'I don't know, General,' he lied. 'Something routine, I should imagine. You know what the base echelon is like?'

'I do,' Bogdan sighed, getting off his horse stiffly. 'All big fat arses, forms and booze on their breath. That reminds me. General Bogdan is thirsty — very thirsty.' He grinned knowingly at York and smacked his cracked lips.

Inwardly York groaned with dismay; the Cossack officer trusted him implicitly and now he was to betray him. Outwardly, however, his face revealed nothing of his inner turmoil. 'I'll see what I can rustle up, General, once we're inside,' he said.

'*Horosho*!' Bogdan boomed. 'Well, don't just stand there, Colonel, lead on.' He grinned in high good humour.

York knocked on the door of the frontier post. 'Come,' a faint voice, which he recognized as that of the Brigadier, answered.

He grasped the brass handle and opened the door.

The Brigadier was seated at a blanket-covered trestle table, his hat removed to reveal that his bald head was startingly white in comparison with his bronzed face. Next to him stood a thin young man with the green and gold flash of the Intelligence Corps on his shoulder, though York guessed he'd be from Field Security too.

'Ah, York,' the Brigadier said, nodding to acknowledge his salute, 'good to see you again.' He saw the two Cossacks standing in the doorway and rose to his feet. 'I see you've brought your friends with you too, eh. Tell the Cossack chappies to sit down. We'll give them a drink to sugar the bitter pill, what.' He grinned at York, showing his big yellow horse teeth.

York translated while the Brigadier fumbled in his pack looking for the whisky. But York noticed that the young Intelligence Corps lieutenant did not move, nor take his cold suspicious eyes off the two Cossacks. His right hand was tensed above the canvas holster of his .38. The lieutenant was obviously expecting trouble.

The Brigadier found the tin mugs and half-filled each with whisky. He handed them to Bogdan and Boris and raised his own in salute, a stupid smile on his face. 'Well, here's to you, *prost*, or whatever they say in German.'

Bogdan raised his mug solemnly in toast, '*Nazostrov* —'

The Russian toast died on his lips. The door had opened behind him and through it York could see six or seven heavily-armed Intelligence Corps sergeants coming out of the back of the truck. But Bogdan's eyes were not on them. They were fixed on the shaven-headed officer standing in the open doorway, dressed in the earth-coloured blouse and breeches of the Red Army, with the heavy gold epaulettes of a senior colonel on his broad shoulders.

'*Treachery, Boris!*' he cried. He sprang to his feet and in that same moment flung the contents of his mug straight into Serov's bulging, triumphant eyes.

Colonel Serov yelped with pain as the whisky struck him full in the face and staggered back, suddenly blinded. Boris' boot slammed into Serov's stomach and the Russian liaison officer crashed against the door. Next instant Boris had bolted through it, followed by Bogdan.

'Stop them!' the Brigadier cried in alarm.

But the Intelligence Corps NCOs were caught by surprise.

The two Cossack officers, striking out wildly on all sides, using their cruelly nailed riding boots to their best advantage, waded through the soldiers. Man after man went down and then they were through running crazily for their grazing horses. 'Out of the bloody way!' the hard-faced Intelligence Corps officer cried, pushing the surprised Brigadier to one side.

'NO!' York screamed.

The lieutenant did not seem to hear. Rigid, taking aim as if he were back on the range, he pressed the .38's trigger. The revolver cracked. The slug whistled through the ranks of the surprised NCOs. Boris faltered in mid-stride. His hands flailed the air wildly. '*General!*' he gasped, staggering forward another pace.

'Boris!' Bogdan stopped a few strides from his stallion.

The little Major waved a suddenly weak hand at the horses. 'Go … go…' Then his legs gave beneath him and he pitched forward on the dusty ground.

When Bogdan turned him over, his stainless steel teeth protruding from his suddenly slack lips, he was dead, a thin trickle of black blood running from the side of his mouth. A moment later a revolver butt crashed into the back of Bogdan's skull and the world went suddenly black.

The trap had been sprung. General Alexei Bogdan was a prisoner again after three years' of freedom.

CHAPTER 6

As pre-arranged, Sergeant Smith opened the Battalion kitchen to the Cossacks. While armed men crouched behind the canvas of each truck, their hands wet with sweat, Smith's cooks laboured over the portable stoves, preparing huge dixies of stew, rice pudding, and tea. Behind them were stacked the fifty litre carboys of cheap red Tyrolean wine that they had brought with them specifically for this meal.

Now it was nearly dark and the suddenly silent and apprehensive Cossacks kept glancing up the road along which their commander had disappeared. A worried Smith knew it was time to serve them the meal and allay their suspicions with hot food, and more importantly, strong wine. He looked at Major Evans, who kept slapping his swagger cane against his brawny leg. 'We're ready with the grub, sir,' he announced. 'I think it's about time —'

'Don't think, Sergeant,' Evans interrupted him, an idiotic smile on his stupid face. 'It's not good for you. Leave that to the officers!' He waved his cane at the group of silent Cossacks closest to the improvised roadside cookhouse. 'All right, feed the brutes.'

Sergeant Smith needed no urging; due to be demobilised in one month's time, he wanted no trouble at this late stage of his Army career. 'All right, my lucky lads,' he yelled at the top of his voice, striking an empty dixie with a ladle to attract the Cossacks' attention, 'come and get it. Lovely grub! Stew and rice pud. Free Army dog biscuits! Wine!' He drew a deep breath and tried in Italian when the Cossacks did not move.

'*Carne ... biscotti ... vino ... Fleisch, Keks ... Wein ... All free, gratis, umsonst...*'

The invitation in Italian and what Sergeant Smith imagined was German had the intended effect. The Cossacks, who had had nothing all day except a handful of cold white beans and water, swarmed forward. Barefoot Cossack women screamed the information to their neighbours. Children whooped with joy. In an instant the silent encampment at the side of the mountain road was transformed into a noisy, hectic chaos.

Jostling each other in unruly queues, the Cossacks fought to obtain a share of the best food they had seen in many a month. Grinning hugely, the sudden tension broken, the cook ladled out portion after portion of the free food, while Sergeant Smith poured the thick red wine into the Russians' canteens. In an instant, the scene resembled a huge picnic, with the Cossacks squatting at the side of the road on their haunches, shouting to one another in extravagant gratitude and exuberance.

Major Evans pushed his way through the Cossacks to where Sergeant-Major Harte, sten gun crooked under his arm, was running his gimlet gaze up and down their ranks, checking for any sign of trouble. 'All right, Harte,' he commanded. 'Stand the men down. I don't think we'll be having any trouble from this little lot. They're too busy feeding their faces.'

Harte looked a little doubtful. All the same he slung his sten gun and began to pass down the trucks, relaying the Major's command in a soft undertone.

But Vera Krasnova, as hungry as the rest of the Cossacks, was unable to eat the food the British gave her. She let the spoonful of thick, hot stew fall back into her canteen untouched.

She felt cold and numbed. The chatter all around her was remote and meaningless. Her mind was too immature to be fully aware of what had happened. Yet all the same she *did* know — instinctively perhaps — that something had happened, or was happening to her beloved General. It was over two hours since he had ridden away with Boris and still he had not returned. She believed too that she had heard a shot, but the older Cossacks had poo-poohed her fears. 'General Bogdan would never let himself be taken,', they had exclaimed confidently. 'He's too old a fox for that, little daughter.'

Vera was not so confident. Now her mind began to stir at last, throwing off its numbness. She dropped her spoon and rose to her feet. Stupidly she wandered through the glowing darkness, her beautiful face illuminated by the flames from the cookhouse fires. Cossacks, who knew her to be Bogdan's mistress, moved out of her way, while the English soldiers stared at her curiously. One or two of them even whistled softly and whispered bawdy remarks out of the sides of their mouths.

She ignored them as she tried to find the officer who had taken charge when the young colonel had left with Bogdan. A sentry said something to her. She shook her head to indicate she did not understand. He put his free hand on her arm. 'Not here, Miss. This is the Major's area.' He tightened his grip, and tried to lead her away.

She was seized by a sudden fury. She tore herself free. Her beautiful face contorted with anger, she rushed by him, ignoring his order to stop, and disappeared into the darkness beyond the truck.

She found Major Evans smoking a cheroot behind one of the trucks, his suede boots propped against its rear wheel, and a large mug of ration rum in his hand. 'Hello, my little chickadee,' he said with surprised delight when he saw the distraught girl, 'and what brings a nice girl like you to my neck of the woods.'

She looked at him in bewilderment. 'Bogdan,' she asked, '*kegir Bogdan?*'

He looked at her blankly. '*Comment?*' he asked in French and now she could see that Major Evans was already pretty drunk.

'*Dov'è il Generale Bogdan?*' she asked in her stumbling Italian.

'*Non capisco,*' he answered. '*Non compris, nicht verstehen.*' He leered at her in the manner of a third-rate villain in a fourth-rate melodrama. 'But they say the language of love is more important than words. '*Come here!*' He grabbed for her waist.

She avoided him easily and he nearly fell over with the momentum of his advance.

'Where is Bogdan?' she cried in Russian desperately.

He laughed crazily, and advanced upon her. Vera backed against the side of the truck panting hard, following him with her eyes like a trapped animal.

'By Christ, you are a pretty little thing,' Evans said and grabbed her.

'*Nyet!*' she screamed.

Evans took no notice. He was breathing very hard now and her nostrils were full of the heavy smell of his hot, rum-tinged breath. He thrust his arms around her and pressed the whole weight of his heavy body against her, so that she could feel the urgency of his desire forced against the softness of her belly.

'*Nyet!*' she cried frantically, as he pushed his knee between her legs and tried to force them apart, his breath coming in shallow, excited gasps.

'It's all right,' he was panting, 'it's all right I'm not going to harm you. It's —'

Major Evans broke off suddenly with a yelp of pain as she freed her right knee and rammed it hard into his crotch. He let go of her at once. His whole body doubled up as he rocked with the burning hurt of it. 'You bitch,' he gasped, his mouth open and gaping like a fish stranded and dying on a river bank, 'you rotten little Russian bitch!'

'*Dov'è il Generale Bogdan?*' she demanded, her voice hard, but the tears streaming silently down her flushed cheeks. Evans, taken up by the burning sick pain in his groin, did not seem to hear.

She repeated her question and to lend emphasis to it she swung her hand across his face.

He cried out in hoarse protest, his dark Welsh eyes blazing with drunken hate. 'I'll tell you where your bloody general is,' he cried. 'He's gone for a Burton, had the chop, turned in his sodding cards. He's dead!'

She stared at him blankly, comprehending neither the Englishman's fury nor his words.

Evans raised himself to his full height, swaying a little with the rum. With relish, he drew his forefinger across his throat in the Italian gesture. Very slowly and clearly he said: 'General bloody Bogdan is dead. *Now do you fucking well understand?*'

CHAPTER 7

Colonel York faced the three of them across the table: the Brigadier, Colonel Serov, and the Intelligence Corps officer who had shot Boris, Major Haig of Field Security. Outside the noise of the reserve battalion, which the Brigadier had brought up to support his own, had died away. They had taken up their positions for the morning and the next phase of Operation Cossack.

York no longer cared what the other three thought of him. Haig was a cold-blooded, unemotional policeman, concerned solely with his duty. The Brigadier was so addle-headed that he was probably not aware of what was really going on; and Serov was in this in order to toady to his political masters in Moscow.

'Gentlemen,' he announced solemnly, eyeing each of their faces in turn in the flickering light of two candles, 'I suggest that we stop this operation now and appeal to the Corps Commander for a review of the whole dirty business.'

There was no reaction to his statement, save that the Major and the shaven-headed Russian turned to stare at the Brigadier. As usual the Brigadier looked puzzled, but he gathered by the fact that the other two were looking at him that he was expected to say something, so he cleared his throat and asked: 'What was that, York?'

The young colonel repeated his statement.

'But, hm, it's already been decided at higher headquarters.'

York restrained his anger. He had to convince Braine in order to prevent the appalling tragedy which he now knew would befall the Cossacks, once they were delivered into Russian hands. The cold-blooded way that Haig had shot Boris in the back showed the sort of treatment they could expect. 'I know, sir,' he said with forced calm. 'But I don't think the Corps Commander was in full possession of all the facts when he made his decision. I know I've only been with the Cossacks for three days myself, but in that time I've discovered the situation wasn't the way it was painted at higher HQ. The Cossacks regard themselves as patriots. They weren't fighting for the Jerries, but *against* the Russian communist government, which they regard as their oppressor.'

Serov shot York a look of pure hatred from those dark bulging eyes of his, but he didn't interrupt the impassioned flow of words.

'I feel, therefore, sir, that if this were known clearly at Corps they could convince London that the Cossacks *are* genuine political refugees who have fled from what they regard as an oppressive, alien government and so deserve the traditional British asylum afforded to political refugees, and not brutal mercenary killers, who fought for the Germans for money.' York paused for breath, telling himself he had never made a speech as long as this in his whole life before. 'I suggest, sir, that we should retain the Cossacks here until we have another decision from Corps.'

For what seemed a long time, no-one reacted to his plea. The Field Security Major looked at his fingernails in obvious boredom. Serov's face revealed nothing, while the Brigadier was clearly struggling to find the words he needed to answer York. Finally he uttered: 'But I say, York, one can't — hm — go about, mucking Corps — hm — around like that, you know. They're busy folk up there. I mean to say!' He said the last words, as if they were explanation enough in themselves.

'But, sir,' York retorted, 'don't you realize that human lives are at stake, not only those of soldiers, but also of old men, women and children? Why do you think von Pannwitz's people fought so violently against repatriation? Because they were so bloody scared of what was waiting for them at Judenburg, they were prepared to tackle British steel with their bare hands, that is why! We can't sully the honour of the British Army like this, with the blood of these people on our hands.'

'Brigadier,' Serov was quicker off the mark than the Brigadier.

'Yes,' Braine said, happy that he was not required to react, 'what is it, Colonel Serov?'

'I'd like to say something about General Bogdan and his Cossacks if I may.'

'Fire away, old chap, do.'

'Thank you.' Serov swung round to look at a red-faced, angry York. 'Colonel York, your sentiments are what one expects from a British gentleman concerned with charity and his honour —'

'Oh, for Christ's sake, get on with it, Serov,' York snapped angrily.

Major Haig looked up from his nails in amusement. In a minute or two, he told himself, the two of them would be going at it hammer and tongs; it would relieve the boredom of the long dull night they had in front of them.

'I will, Colonel York. But do you really think that it is worth wasting your charity and your honour on such people? Are they really the innocents you make them out to be? I shall answer that question for you. They are not. No,' his voice rose firmly, knowing that one day this little speech of his would find its way to Marshal Stalin's ears, 'the men you are trying to protect from Soviet justice are not only traitors to their Fatherland, they are also cold-blooded murderers.'

'We only have your word for it, Serov,' York shot back. 'You can tell us anything you like about what happened in Russia during the war.'

'I'm not talking about Russia,' Serov answered.

'What are you talking about then, Serov?'

'Here — Italy,' Serov said with a note of triumph in his voice.

'I don't quite follow,' the Brigadier interrupted. 'Could you — hm — explain, Colonel Serov?'

'With pleasure.' Serov fumbled inside his Red Army blouse, decorated solely with the cheap enamel of the Order of the Red Banner, and pulled out a dirty envelope. He passed it to Braine, saying: 'Perhaps you would care to look at the two photographs it contains, sir.'

Puzzled, the Brigadier opened the flap and then gasped. 'I say, where ... where did you get these, Serov?'

'From the US Army Signal Corps,' Serov announced, drawing out the words significantly. 'They were taken in the first week of May in the US Fifth Army area by their official photographers. The men in question — a sergeant and a captain — belonged to the US Tenth Mountain Division.'

'But what are they?' York demanded, 'and what have they got to do with the Black Cossacks?'

'Yes, Serov, what indeed?' the Brigadier drew his eyes away from the ghastly photos and added his voice to Colonel York's.

'They were taken, Brigadier, after the Tenth came into contact with those famed noble Cossacks of Colonel York here.'

York flushed crimson. 'Let me have a look at the damned things!'

Silently the Brigadier pushed the photographs across the table to him. Hastily York held them up to the poor light of the guttering candles and recoiled. 'My God,' he whispered. '*Not that*!'

Each photograph showed a man in the olive-drab of the US Army sprawled in the extravagant pose of violent death; and in each case, where the man's eyes had once been, there were gaping empty sockets.

'Yes, Colonel York,' Serov pressed home his attack. 'Done by Bogdan's Cossacks. Done in Italy, against troops of our Allies, carried out in the usual gentlemanly Cossack fashion against helpless prisoners.' He smiled coldly. 'And those are the noble soldiers you are trying to protect from Soviet justice, York!'

The young British colonel said nothing.

Serov turned to Brigadier Braine once more. 'Sir, I was in touch with General Mark Clark yesterday to inform him that the British Army was in the process of arresting the Cossacks so that they could be handed over to the Soviet authorities and he congratulated me — and you naturally too. He also gave me a message which he asked should be passed on to the British commander in charge — you, Brigadier.

'He expressed the wish that not one of the Cossack criminals who mutilated his men in May should escape justice. Indeed, if I can quote him in my poor English, he said: "I'd personally like to string up every last one of the sons of bitches".'

'I don't know — hm — about stringing up, but you and General Clark can — hm — rest assured that the British Army will carry out its agreement to see that these Cossack chaps are handed over to the Red Army.'

Serov glanced maliciously at York and said, 'I knew all along, Brigadier, that the British Army would not go back on its word.'

For the first time since the discussion began, the Major from Field Security spoke, 'Gentlemen,' he said easily, rising to his feet with a yawn, 'I think we've talked enough, don't you? What about a spot of shut-eye before tomorrow? It's going to be a long, hot day, don't you think?'

The Brigadier yawned too, grateful that this interruption was bringing the unpleasant, puzzling business to an end. 'Yes, I think you're right, Major. We'll all need as much rest as we can get.' He rose to his feet, put on his beret and touched his Eighth Army fly-whisk to it casually. 'Well, good night then, chaps.'

'Good night, sir,' they replied in unison.

Serov and the Field Security Major followed, leaving York standing alone, staring numbly at his own flickering distorted shadow on the wall, knowing that he had failed.

CHAPTER 8

Bogdan woke with a groan. Pain stabbed hot in his right eyeball. He opened his eyes and a vice seemed to squeeze cruelly at the back of his head. Gingerly, his eyes closed again, he felt his skull. His black hair was matted with dried blood.

Then he remembered. How they had been tricked by the young British colonel; how Boris had been shot down in cold blood; how he had been beaten to the ground. Bogdan groaned again, but this time not with pain, but at the overwhelming knowledge that he had been betrayed after all, and that now his Black Cossacks were on the other side of the frontier in partisan country, leaderless apart from a few young, inexperienced *sotniks*.

Painfully he raised himself onto one elbow. His nostrils were assailed by the odour of disinfectant and the sharp bite of ether. He realized suddenly that he was in some sort of hospital. He blinked his eyes a couple of times and tried to make out the room, illuminated by the pale gleam of the moon through the barred window to the right of his bed. There was a white table to the left of his cot, littered with dirty swabs of cotton wool. His gaze swept past the wooden crucifix on the otherwise bare wall — probably he was in a civilian hospital then — to the first door; and from there to the second one next to the room's solitary chair. Gingerly, Bogdan raised himself from the bed, noting automatically that they had taken his boots and pistol, and tip-toed to the first door. Ignoring the painful throbbing at his temples, he tried the metal handle cautiously, ear pressed to the door for the slightest sound. The handle moved easily. But the door did not open. It was locked from the outside!

Bogdan bent and peered at the crack beneath the door. The light was on in the corridor outside and on the opposite wall he just could make out two thin shadows and a thicker one between them: the outline of two chair legs and what must be feet. They had posted a sentry outside.

Cautiously, his bare feet making a slight sticking sound on the polished wooden floor, he padded back to the window. Grabbing two of the iron bars, he heaved with all his strength but to no avail. The window was securely barred. There was no way of escape by that means.

He had to get out and save his people. *But how?* He looked at the other door. Obviously it did not lead to the corridor. He guessed it led to a bathroom. The question was — did it have an outside window and was that window barred?

He cocked his head to one side. The sentry out there was asleep, for he could just make out his soft regular breathing. Swiftly he opened the other door and found himself, as he had expected, in a bathroom.

His eyes took in the little room at a glance — the chipped bath, the lavatory, the white cabinet on the wall and the tiny window, barred as heavily as the main one. '*Damn … damn … damn!*' he cursed to himself, closing the door behind him so that he could switch on the light without fear of detection.

For a long time, he simply stood there in his bare feet, staring blankly at the wall opposite wondering what he should do next. From outside there came no sound, save that of the wind in the trees and the forlorn cry of a night bird.

He walked over to the little cabinet and opened it A couple of rolls of paper bandage, stamped with the eagle and swastika of the *Wehrmacht*, two empty bottles, labelled '*grippe*,' and a wire bandage clamp were all the cupboard contained. Nothing he could use to free himself: no weapon to attack the sentry, no tool to break through the window bars.

Morosely he stared round the room, looking for inspiration. Then he had it — the bath!

Hastily he dropped to his knees and examined the area around the little brass grid, which covered the waste pipe leading from the bath. The wooden floor there was damp and soft. He crossed to the cupboard again and snatched the clamp. With his powerful hands, he bent it into shape and picked at the little brass grid. It came off quite easily and the floor was flooded with a miniature fountain of soap-suds and disinfectant.

Thrusting one hand into the opening, he heaved. The pipe did not move. With a stifled grunt, he heaved again. This time it gave. He disengaged his fist and moved the pipe to one side so that he could see into the hole beneath the floorboards.

He had guessed rightly. He was on the ground floor. Beneath him, barely visible in the weak light from the single bulb above him, he could just make out the damp black earth below. Beneath the bathroom was a space, perhaps a metre broad. Definitely broad enough for his body. How was he to get into it?

He retraced his steps to the main door. The sentry was still breathing softly. Satisfied, he returned to the bathroom and locked the door gently behind him. He took the two rolls of paper bandage from the little cabinet and unrolling them used them to plug the door, pressing the thick crepe paper carefully around the crack in the hope that it would help to deaden the noise he would soon have to make.

Bogdan now looked at the area of woodwork around the drainage pipe hole. He would have to extend it at least another

159

thirty centimetres in order to get to the hollow below. But how? He had no tools, save his bare hands.

Suddenly he had it. He ripped at the silver decorative bullet that fitted into the first pouch of his *Cherkasska*. With all his strength, he scored a deep line in the wet, pulpy plank. Time and time again, the sweat standing out on his forehead, he repeated the operation until he was satisfied that the scored line was deep enough. Taking off his thick black coat he laid it carefully over the end of the plank and crashed home his heel.

The plank splintered and cracked like an exploding 88mm shell. He tensed, his bare foot raised absurdly in the air, his heart beating furiously, as he waited for the anticipated cry of rage and the angry beating on the locked door. Nothing happened. The sentry had not heard.

Removing his coat he wrenched the end of the broken plank free and repeated the operation. Thirty minutes later, his heel bruised a deep blue, he had completed the task. Below him he had exposed a jagged hole big enough to squeeze through.

Grabbing his bloodstained coat, he dropped it into the hollow below the cracked floorboards. Taking a deep breath, he lowered himself after it, inching by the jagged ends of the wood by a fraction. He had done it!

What followed was a confusion of pipes, dripping stench and slime, and a passage of unutterable darkness. Twice he ran into a rough wall and thought himself trapped for good. But a frenzy of fumbling in the inky blackness revealed to him that the passage continued.

There were rats everywhere. They scattered in green-eyed panic before him, re-forming instantly like a horrid grey carpet once he had passed. He ignored them, fighting back his horror of this nightmarish underground world, telling himself he must not panic — there *had* to be a way out.

Now his head began to ring. Not only from the blow he had received but from the gas that filled the passage. Time and again, he shook his head, trying to drive away the strange torpor that was threatening to overcome him.

He blundered on, his body bent double, the rough stone tearing the skin of his shoulders cruelly, trying not to breathe too deeply in the fetid atmosphere.

It seemed an eternity before he noticed that the air now playing on his face was gradually becoming cooler and fresher. His head started to clear. He halted for an instant and turned his face from left to right. There was a cooler current on his right cheek. Blindly he stumbled on, his hand outstretched in front of him, palm upright so that he could feel the cooler air playing on it and guide himself to its source.

He blundered into another damp wall. For a moment he thought his progress was blocked once more but he groped along its rough surface, feeling the air increasingly cooler on his hands. His fingers fumbled against a rusty hinge. His heart leapt. An air vent perhaps. His hand knocked a catch. Eagerly he seized it and tugged hard. Something gave with a rusty squeak. Damp night air streamed in and suddenly he could see the dark spiked outline of firs high above his head. He had opened a door to the grounds!

Swiftly he lay down and thrust both arms through the little door. Breathing in hard and trying to make himself as small as possible, he began to wriggle his way through, feeling the wet grass brushing against his flushed face.

Then he was through and the dampness was penetrating his uniform. Gratefully he lay there, taking deep gulps of the night air, savouring its freshness, allowing his eyes to become accustomed to the darkness, trying to take his bearings.

But time was running out. From somewhere within the hospital, there came a muffled cry of alarm. Lights began to go on everywhere. He staggered to his feet. A window was flung open. Someone shouted something — some sort of alarm for other soldiers. He propelled himself to his feet.

'*Halt!*' a harsh voice commanded in German, '*oder ich schiesse — halt!*'

He dived forward, body doubled up, running swiftly across the dew damp lawn towards the cover of the firs. Behind him scarlet flame stabbed the air. The explosion of a heavy automatic. A bullet whined off the stone wall of an outhouse just in front of him, Bogdan zig-zagged to the left. Just in time. A machine pistol opened up with a vicious hiss. Tracer filled the darkness like pink and white morse just where he had been.

The firs loomed up in front of him. 'He's heading for the trees!' a voice cried to his right. His bare bleeding feet flew across the grass. The trees were only ten metres away now. The machine pistol chattered again. Something red-hot struck him in the right shoulder. He yelped with pain and staggered on blindly, the blood streaming down his suddenly numb arm. The pines lashed cruelly against his face. Behind him the cries and shouts of anger grew increasingly faint. He stumbled on. On and on, plunging ever deeper into the cover of the firs.

How long he ran he did not know. Once he crossed a narrow gravelled road, gleaming in the moonlight. For a moment he was tempted to follow it to get back to his Cossacks. But the rattle of tracks warned him of danger in time. He ducked back into the firs. A little British Bren carrier came squarely around the bend, soldiers standing upright in its back, flashing their torches into the ditches to left and right.

Bogdan pressed himself to the wet earth. The lights flashed through the foliage above him. Out of the comer of his eye, he caught a glimpse of them moving up the road. Then the carrier disappeared round the next bend.

This narrow escape gave Bogdan the direction he needed. Assuming that the British would think he would attempt to get back to his Division and would naturally block that direction, he guessed the road taken by the carrier would lead to the frontier and the Black Cossacks. Accordingly he began to work his way through the firs on a course parallel to the little country road.

His body racked with pain from the bullet in his shoulder, General Bogdan staggered southwards, one overwhelming thought dominating everything else: he must reach the Division before dawn when the British would act. *He must*!

CHAPTER 9

With the black wall of the Alps rising behind them like a menacing backdrop, the soldiers waited in numb silence, their faces coloured by the rising sun. No orders came. The NCOs smoked quietly, coughing drily every now and again as men do at dawn, their throats irritated by the first cigarette of the day.

Along the road the Cossacks were beginning to wake now. Men relieved themselves against the rock wall, women hushed irritable children and began to scout around for wood to light their cooking fires. The animation of the previous evening had vanished and if they looked at the long lines of freshly shaven and washed soldiers at all, their faces were sullen and heavy with suspicion. Six of Sergeant Smith's cooks filed over to them to deliver boxes of compo rations to feed the women and children. But a young Cossack *sotnik*, who seemed to have assumed command since Bogdan had departed, shouted angrily at the leading man in broken German and told him the Cossacks didn't want their rations. Puzzled and a little angry, the cooks turned and trooped back.

Sergeant-Major Harte watching the little scene turned to Major Evans, standing next to Colonel York, and remarked: 'Looks as if it's going to be a bit dicey, sir. Hope they'll keep their hair on, sir.'

Evans grinned hugely at the prospect of a bit of action and said loudly for York's benefit. 'They'd better, Sarnt-Major, or they're going to get a bloody nose, eh, Colonel?'

York turned and looked at Evans coldly. 'You can brief the men now, Evans,' he said icy-voiced.

'Sir!'

Together with the Sergeant-Major, Evans strode across to the waiting men. 'All right, you lot, get them fags out,' Harte snarled. 'And you, you idle man there in the rear rank, get yer flies done up, or yer'll be flashing yer Hampton next!'

Evans issued instructions. 'At zero seven, we move in. Each platoon will take up its allotted position, breaking 'em up into manageable groups. We move over the border, where the trains will be waiting. I don't expect they'll give us any trouble, now that we've got their General in the bag and his second in command. But if there is, shoot to kill!' Evans savoured the phrase with obvious relish.

Behind him, York bit his lip and turned away, as if he were trying to blot out the whole scene.

'If any of their officers attempt to commit suicide,' Evans went on, 'you will stop them doing so. If there is the slightest danger to our own men, you'll allow the buggers to get on with it. One less for the Russkis to have to deal with, eh?' he grinned at the men. 'Sarnt-Major, stand 'em down till zero seven and tell the cooks that they can dish out the rum ration now.'

As Evans, obviously highly pleased with himself, strolled back to York, the men looked at one another. Since the end of the war there had not been one issue of ration rum, and even during it they had only received their half mugful when they were about to go into action. Did this mean, 'Mad Mike' was going to get them into trouble — again?

'Sod this for a lark,' Sergeant Smith cursed to himself, as he began to hand over the big carboys of issue rum to the platoon representatives. 'Doesn't he know I'm gonna be demobbed next month?'

Bogdan halted, leaning against the rock wall for support. The blood had stopped flowing from his wounded arm, but his naked feet, ripped and torn by the rough surface of the track, were bleeding freely. Bogdan did not notice them, however. His whole attention was concentrated on the frontier.

Smoke was now coming in a thin blue curl from the chimney of the frontier hut in which he and Boris had been trapped the previous evening. He guessed the British were cooking their breakfast. Some five hundred metres beyond in a large gap in the rock face — perhaps some quarry or other — neat rows of khaki-coloured tents had been pitched. Obviously more British troops to reinforce those escorting the Cossacks on the Italian side of the border. Down on the frontier road itself, there was only the elderly Austrian policeman who had been there before. But now, in addition to his club, he had a British sten gun slung over his stooped shoulder.

With a bit of luck he could deal with the policeman and be across before the alarm was raised. There was no other way. On both sides of the little frontier road, the walls of the pass rose too steeply for him to tackle them in his present condition. He took a deep breath, and moved down onto the road, his feet leaving a bloody imprint on the dust.

Now he was twenty metres away from the lone policeman. In the first blood-red rays of the rising sun, he could make out every detail of the man's shabby uniform, down to the darker outline of the eagle and swastika which had been removed from his upper right sleeve at the end of the war. Cautiously, his face contorted with pain, Bogdan advanced on the unsuspecting man, ready to choke the life out of him before he could raise the alarm.

Ten metres. In another moment he would have him and he'd be armed too — with the policeman's sten — ready to fight his way through to his own people. Flexing the stiff muscles of his wounded shoulder and feeling the dried blood crack on his skin, he prepared for the attack.

His right foot suddenly struck a sharp flint hidden in the white dust. The agony was too much for him. Bogdan could not repress a yelp of pain. The policeman spun round with surprising speed for such an elderly man, the sten clenched in both hands and pointing straight at Bogdan's stomach.

'*Haende hoch*!' he commanded, his wrinkled face blanched with fear, as he realized that this gigantic figure in a bloodstained coat had been about to kill him. With a groan, Bogdan raised his hands, swamped by a feeling of absolute defeat.

Cautiously the policeman approached him, ran his eyes up and down the front of Bogdan's tattered uniform and then frisked him with his one free hand. Satisfied that the Cossack had no weapons hidden on his person, he faced Bogdan again and said: 'Are you the Cossack General the Tommies brought over last night?'

Bogdan nodded glumly, not trusting himself to speak.

'You know what they're' — he indicated the British tents — 'going to do with your people?'

'No.'

'They've got the trains waiting for them at Mauthen. From there it's east to Villach and up to —' the policeman shrugged his skinny shoulders. 'You know the rest?'

'Judenburg?' Bogdan croaked.

'*Jawohl*. Judenburg and the Ivans.'

'*Boshe moi*!' Bogdan cursed in Russian. Desperately he cried. 'Let me through.'

The policeman hesitated. 'My lad was at Stalingrad,' he said suddenly.

Bogdan looked at him blankly.

The policeman saw the look. 'He came back all right,' he explained. 'But minus his eyes. Like a baby again he is. His mother has to do everything for him these days. Just like the little baby he once was.'

'How old is he?' Bogdan forced himself to ask.

'Twenty. He was only eighteen when they sent him to Stalingrad with the *Hoch-und Deutschmeister*. Eighteen.' Suddenly tears began to trickle down the policeman's leathery cheeks. The sten trembled in his hands. Twice the policeman forced himself to keep the machine pistol levelled at the big Russian; then he said: 'Go on, Cossack — run for it. And God bless you!'

Bogdan did not need a second invitation. 'Thank you,' he cried hoarsely and began to move down the road into Italy, leaving the Austrian policeman behind him, staring wet-eyed into eternity, the tears streaming down his face unheeded.

Punctually at seven o'clock, the infantry moved forward, every other man carrying a length of barbed wire which was attached to the soldier holding a weapon in front. Thus they formed a kind of armed fence. Swifty the grim-faced British platoon broke the Cossack column into individual, manageable units, each one hemmed in and separate from the rest by the human hurdles.

Immediately, the Cossacks reacted. At first, led by a white-bearded patriarch, they sang the traditional 'Our Father' and 'Save Thy People, O Lord' in their deep voices, accompanied hesitantly by the anxious piping of the children and the weeping women. But as the various platoons began to hustle them forward towards the frontier, angry shouting and cursing broke out on all sides.

The infantrymen, who were not holding the barbed wire, jabbed at the Cossacks with their bayonets, Reluctantly they started to move forward. Here and there bolder spirits dropped to the ground and tried to escape through the legs of the advancing British, allowing the moving fence to pass by them.

But Major Evans was prepared for that eventuality. Standing on a height overlooking the whole length of the road, he ordered his 'goon squads' into action: six-man patrols, armed with pick handles, who followed the infantry, cracking the heads of the would-be escapers and forcing them back into the boxed-up groups. One or two who refused to flee were beaten insensibly and left lying in the dust for the trucks to pick up. Slowly but surely, the column began to advance to the frontier.

'Take a gander at that, sir,' Evans chortled exuberantly, 'now the buggers are really moving!' He shouted through his megaphone to the lone figure of Sergeant-Major Harte whose face was set in a look of disgust: 'Sarnt-Major, double 'em up there! Get 'em to open their legs — nothing will fall out!'

'Sir!' Harte yelled back without turning to look at the height, and snapped out fresh orders.

'You're enjoying this, aren't you, Evans?' York said in disgust, watching the panic-stricken women and children forced into a shambling run by the infantry with their bayonets and telling himself that the York and Lancs Regiment had never done anything as shameful as this in their history.

'Of course, great fun, sir!' Evans bellowed back above the cries. 'Peacetime was beginning to become a bit of a ruddy bore. This is some sort of action at least.'

Full of self-loathing, York snapped: 'And what do you do when they start to use their own weapons, Major?' Evans, his dark Welsh eyes sparkling excitedly, spun round. 'They haven't got the spunk for that, sir. Without that ruffian of a general of theirs they're lost. Now we've got them in the palm of our hands.' He crushed his own big hands together dramatically, his heavy Celtic jaw set, as if he were physically mashing the fleeing Cossacks in it. 'They've had it … we've got 'em by the short and curlies…'

Vera shambled forward with the rest of the panic-stricken, weeping women and their screaming children. Her face was taut with incredulity and shock. Her once beautiful cheeks were slack and ugly, her dark eyes wide and staring.

A British soldier, bayonet held in front of him, jabbed at her and forced her on. She lost a shoe. But there was no chance of picking it up. The mob pushed her onwards. She kicked off the other and stumbled on, the pebbles of the little mountain road cutting cruelly into the soles of her feet.

Ahead of her the red and white striped barrier splintered and smashed under the weight of Cossack bodies. Men and women went down by the score, but the British urged them to their feet again, striking them with their cruel sticks, prodding them with their bayonets. A child fell and in an instant it was submerged and trampled on by the panic-stricken crowd. A couple of British soldiers dropped their wire hurdles and tried to rescue the fallen child. To no avail. They, too, were swept forward like flotsam carried by the irresistible force of the tide.

Vera caught a glimpse of a bloody face, a head twisted at the awkward angle of death under her feet. The sight broke through her frightened numbness. She raised her head and howling like a wild animal, she screamed: 'Where is the General?… *Oh, my God, save us Bogdan!*'

The plea was taken up on all sides. The narrow stone chasm was filled with that desperate cry: '*Save us Bogdan…*'

CHAPTER 10

'*COSSACKS!*' the tremendous cry echoed and re-echoed from the rocks. '*BLACK COSSACKS, I AM HERE!*'

Evans, still supervising the operation from his position on the height, swung round: 'Christ, it's him!' In a flash he drew his pistol and fired. The bullet exploded in a flurry of angry blue sparks at Bogdan's feet and went howling into nothing.

'Stop that, you bloody fool!' York cried. With an angry blow, he knocked Evans' revolver upwards, just as he was about to fire at the swaying yet magnificent figure opposite them on the height which commanded the other side of the frontier road.

Bogdan ignored both the bullet and York's attempt to save his life; he did not seem to see the two British officers. Instead his great chest swelled out as he commanded, '*BLACK COSSACKS-TO YOUR WEAPONS!*'

'*To the weapons!*' the answering cry rose everywhere from thousands of hoarse throats.

In an instant the young Cossacks started to pull out their hidden weapons, while the older men, lacking firearms, grabbed their clubs and knives. Suddenly the surprised infantrymen were confronted with an armed mob, the young men facing them in grim determination, the women and children suddenly weeping no longer, their tear-stained faces transformed with new hope. Here and there an NCO or soldier raised his weapon, as if he were about to fire. But the look on the faces of the Cossacks soon dissuaded him.

'By Christ, the treacherous buggers had weapons all along!' Evans gasped. 'But I'll show them!'

'You'll do what?' York rapped, new hope in his heart. 'Do you want to cause a massacre? What about our own men? A lot of them are going to get hurt if anything starts down there. It'll be hand to hand fighting, with the advantage on the Cossacks' side.' Suddenly he forgot Evans. Cupping his hands around his mouth, he shouted in German, 'General, what do you hope to achieve?'

Bogdan looked across at him, his shoulders bowed with pain and exhaustion, his wounded arm hanging limply by the side of his ragged, bloody *cherkasska*, but still every inch the proud commander of the Black Cossacks. 'Freedom!' he cried back. 'Freedom for my people!'

'General, I'd like to give you it. From the bottom of my heart, I would. But it is impossible. Your fate has already been decided in Moscow and London. You must be handed over.' York knew after his experiences of the previous night, there was no point in lying to Bogdan now; he knew exactly why the Black Cossacks were being moved into Austria. They were being repatriated.

'Nothing is impossible!' Bogdan roared back. 'My people *must* be freed!'

A great roar of affirmation rose from the Cossacks. 'The Black Cossacks must be freed!'

York did not look round, but hissed at Evans, 'For Chrissake get on the Eighteen Set and raise the Brigadier.'

'What for?' Evans asked sullenly. 'What the hell can he do?'

'Shut up!' York snapped. 'Tell him I need air — and I need it urgently.'

'But fighters couldn't —'

'Spotter planes would do,' York interrupted. 'But tell him anything with wings.'

'What if he asks why?' Evans protested, fumbling already with the earphones of the radio transmitter. 'I mean he's just over the hills waiting for us to show up with Cossacks at this very moment.'

'I don't care if he's waiting in bloody Timbuctoo,' York snapped. 'Just tell him this, that if we don't have air to impress those Cossacks down there, the Brigade's going to have a massacre on its hands...'

Swiftly the handful of young *sotniks* clambered up the rock face to their commander, as the British infantry watched impotently, while they waited for orders from a perplexed Colonel York. One Cossack caught Bogdan just as he was beginning to sway backwards with exhaustion. Hastily another of the young officers unscrewed his flask of fiery Italian *grappa* and forced a couple of drops through the General's teeth. He coughed and the colour flooded back to his face.

He straightened up and looked across at the slim, tense English colonel standing on the height opposite him, while below the Tommies and his own Cossacks looked from one to another, wondering what the outcome of this strange duel would be. 'Colonel York,' Bogdan began, his voice firmer and more commanding than ever, 'I shall give you thirty minutes to make your decision. We either leave here alive, or we fight — and possibly die.' He hesitated for only a fraction of a second. 'But if many of my Cossacks die, so will your soldiers as well.'

'We do not want to fight, General,' York yelled back hastily. 'We can settle this by peaceful means. You must surrender first and then we will ensure that the case of the Black Cossack Division is reviewed once more. I promise you — on my word as a British officer...' He stopped short, realizing that he had used that fatal phrase once before.

Bogdan looked at the Colonel's suddenly bowed head and in a way felt sorry for him. He knew York to be an honest man, forced to carry out orders that were repugnant to him. But he had no time now for the Englishman's moral dilemma. Somehow or other he must save his people from what was waiting for them in Austria. He looked down at Vera, her hair bedraggled, her dress ripped to reveal those wonderful breasts. He must not let her, and all the women and children grouped around her, suffer the same fate his own Vera and all the many other Veras of the Great Purges of the thirties had suffered. She must not become one of those toothless, prematurely grey whores of the labour camps in Siberia, whose only escape from the unbearable misery of their existence had been suicide or death from exhaustion.

While Evans worked frantically with the little radio, which had a range of only a few miles, York returned to the attack. 'General Bogdan,' he called, his voice echoing back and forth in the stone canyon which had grown suddenly very silent, 'where would you hope to go, even if I did allow you to move on? There is no place for you in Europe.'

'If Europe doesn't want us,' Bogdan answered, clutching at straws, thinking mistakenly that perhaps the British colonel was beginning to weaken, 'then there are other places. After the First World War, the Allies shipped our Cossack forefathers to Africa and South America. You could do the same now.'

'Impossible, General. Times have changed. The Africans have their own ideas these days.' Desperately York babbled on, while the crowds below watched, only half understanding the rapid flow of words in the foreign tongue, and while York himself listened to Evans' hurried attempts to raise the Brigadier. And then he had him! 'Sir, we need air immediately. A bad situation has arisen here.'

Evans was silent, while the Brigadier asked his usual puzzled questions, then he was saying urgently, 'All right, sir. Thank you, sir. We'll be keeping a sharp look out for them. *Over!*'

York heaved a sigh of relief, only half hearing Bogdan's shout that he had 'exactly twenty minutes left'.

Bogdan started. Painfully, feeling the throb of the wound in his shoulder acutely, he turned to the north, the direction from which the new sound was coming.

'Five minutes to go, General,' the *sotnik* who had offered him the *grappa* said, looking at his wrist watch.

Bogdan did not react. He was staring at the three black dots clearly outlined against the hard blue of the morning sky. Down below the Cossacks had begun to look in the same direction, their faces suddenly pale and apprehensive.

'Planes!' Bogdan broke the heavy frightened silence. 'They're bringing up planes!'

'The English bastards,' a *sotnik* cursed furiously. 'But surely they wouldn't use planes against innocent men and women, General?'

Bogdan did not answer. His gaze was fixed on the three single-winged planes with the red and white roundel under their wings as they hurried ever closer, coming down low so that it appeared they were just skimming over the top of the heights. And then they were there, drowning all other sound with their ear-splitting roar. For an instant the upturned faces were blackened by the great shadows they trailed after them and next moment they were soaring high into the sky once more, leaving the valley resounding to their roar.

'General!'

It was York.

'What do you want?' Bogdan yelled, his brain racing, wondering urgently whether the British would dare to use planes against them.

'What you just saw, General, were our spotter planes. They are simply a warning.'

'A warning of what?'

'A warning that bombers will follow if you don't surrender.'

'But your bombs would hit your own soldiers!'

'A couple of blasts on my whistle and they will withdraw to safety leaving you and your people to face the full might of our bombers.'

'But the women and children!' Bogdan protested desperately, his nerve beginning to crack. 'You wouldn't kill innocent women and children ... would you?' he added weakly.

York hesitated for an instant. Even the new Labour government in London would not go *that* far in their attempts to appease Moscow. The press would slaughter it and hound it out of office within a week. He knew that, but Bogdan, a man used to totalitarian terror, did not. 'Yes,' he said firmly. 'If needs be, General Bogdan, I'm prepared to order the bombers to attack your column. The Black Cossacks must obey my commands.'

Bogdan looked down at the women and children below and yielded. He couldn't risk their lives. His Cossacks were soldiers. They were used to chancing everything in seemingly hopeless ventures. But not their women and children.

'General, let us go down fighting,' a young *sotnik* urged. 'Die we must — one way or the other.'

Sadly Bogdan shook his head, his heart too full to allow him to answer.

'Well?' York demanded, pressing home his advantage. 'What is it to be, General?'

Above his head, the three L-5s came hurtling in again, skimming over the heads of the crowd in an alarming flurry of sound. Men ducked instinctively and children whimpered with terror. Bogdan caught a glimpse of Vera's frightened face. He swallowed hard. 'Colonel, there is no alternative,' he replied, finding it difficult to select the words he needed. 'I... I surrender the Black Cossack Division to you. But —'

'Yes?'

'You must not let the women and children go back, you know where?'

'What do you mean?'

'Colonel, in a moment, I shall order my Cossacks to drop their weapons and proceed without any further trouble. You have *my* word as a Cossack officer on that.'

York flushed, but said nothing.

'I shall lead them personally. But save our womenfolk. Don't hand them over to the Reds.' Bogdan's face contorted desperately. 'Give us that little comfort, then we may die happy... Please, I ... I beg you!' he held up his clasped hands in the classic posture of supplication.

York looked away for an instant, unable to bear the sight of the great Cossack General's humiliation.

'But we can't do that, Colonel,' Evans objected. 'The agreement states —'

'Will you shut your damn fool mouth,' York cut in savagely.

'General Bogdan, the women and children can accompany you to the trains. Then you go the rest of the way alone,' he faltered, unable to say more.

'Thank you ... thank you from the bottom of my heart, Colonel,' Bogdan called back.

A moment later he was helped down the steep side of the height by his young officers like the weak, beaten old man he was.

CHAPTER 11

With a metallic clatter of steel wheels, the smoke dying at its funnel, the first of the trains came to a halt in the village station, momentarily shrouding it in its sad grey fog. The train, like those which would follow it to take the men across the Demarcation Line, had been specially prepared by the Royal Engineers. All metal objects had been removed from the wooden-benched carriages, in case the deportees used them as weapons. The windows had been covered with heavy wire grilles to prevent them from jumping out and a barbed wire hurdle had been erected behind the coal tender so that no one could attempt to take over the locomotive. And at the end of the long line of carriages, bearing the fading legend '*Deutsche Reichsbahn*', there was a carriage the windows of which were blacked out and from which came the biting odour of chemicals. It was the mortuary van, intended for those who would undoubtedly commit suicide during the long journey to Judenburg.

But the Cossacks, knowing the hopelessness of their position, were already doing that before they were forced aboard the train. A *sotnik* was already dead, hanging from the chain in the station's little lavatory, his face a hideous purple, his tongue hanging out of his gaping mouth like a dirty rag. Mishka, Bogdan's groom, lay behind an outhouse, his wrists slit with a sharp-edged can of 'M & V', once given to him by his 'friend' Sergeant Smith of the cooks. Wherever they could elude detection, away from their British guards, Cossacks swiftly carried out their acts of self-destruction.

Twice an increasingly angry Brigadier Braine ordered Bogdan to command his men to stop 'this nonsense'. But Bogdan only shook his head and refused. 'My God,' York added his protests to those of the Brigadier, 'but you must do something, General,' he said desperately. 'They're killing themselves indiscriminately. Think of the effect on the women and children.'

Bogdan was now very weak, but still in control of himself. Supported by Vera's arm, he looked at York and replied: 'Let them see how their people once suffered here, Colonel. Let them remember how terrible this place was.'

'But not this! Surely you don't want *children* to remember these terrible things, General!' York objected fervently.

Bogdan saw that the British were beginning to move the first of his Cossacks into the train and waved the Colonel aside, saying, 'Let me have a moment now, please.' He turned to Vera. 'My daughter,' he said gently, stroking her pale, drawn face, 'an end has come.'

'No!' She clung to him desperately, her hands wet with blood from the freshly opened shoulder wound. 'No, Alexei, don't let them take you.'

He looked down at her with the compassion and gentleness of one who no longer belonged to this world, one who viewed it with the detachment of the already dead. 'I must go with my Black Cossacks. I led them in victory; now I must lead them in defeat.'

'You go to your death, Alexei.' She clutched at him in passionate anger. 'Don't you realize that — *to your death!*'

'Yes,' he answered simply. 'But when I am dead, Vera, when you are safe away from this terrible, blood-stained Europe, remember me and the Black Cossacks.' For a moment he had a sudden vision of her in the years to come, speaking another language to people who would never understand the kind of world into which they had been born. There would be other men, of course. Other lips would kiss her lips, other hands would fondle her breasts.

'One day, Vera, you must speak.'

'Speak of what, Alexei?'

'Speak of such people as the Black Cossacks — say that we existed. Relate what we fought for.' His voice grew firmer, with some of that old command and harshness in it. 'Relate what we died for?'

'No, not die, Alexei,' her voice faltered. 'Not die.'

Bogdan did not seem to hear. Nor did he see how Cossack after Cossack was torn from the arms of his wailing family and bundled into the train, the steam hissing from its metal sides as if with increasing impatience. His eyes were fixed on some more distant horizon, known only to him. 'Not yet, little daughter, not yet. But one day there will be somebody who will listen to your story. A writer perhaps, prepared to take up an unpopular cause. Or perhaps one who wants to embarrass governments, create a little sensation that will last a few days.' He shrugged and winced with pain. 'Who knows what kind of man he will be? But there will be one, and to him you will relate the story of General Bogdan and his Black Cossacks. Promise me, little daughter!' He looked down at her. 'Promise!'

She nodded numbly, unable to speak, the tears streaming unchecked down her face.

'Good,' Bogdan said satisfied. He turned his gaze to the long train. It was packed with his Cossacks now. He stared at their honest peasant faces and wondered how many of them would ever again see their Quiet Don, when all the torture, the executions, the long years in prison were over. Few, he told himself sadly. There had been no hope right from the start.

They had blinded themselves to the truth — that there was no regaining the past just because they desired it. He laughed suddenly — a bitter, cynical little sound.

Vera looked at him, the tears streaming down her face, but did not speak. Colonel York, his whole body tense and barely under control, asked: 'What is it, General?'

'I was just thinking of what Boris once said to me.'

Across the track, the Brigadier on the platform was waving to indicate that York should order Bogdan onto the waiting train.

'He once said that you could find sympathy only in the dictionary. Between shit and syphilis!' Bogdan laughed again and then he saw the Brigadier's angry waving. 'I think I must go.'

'*No!*' Vera screamed.

Gently but firmly, Bogdan freed himself from her frantic grip. 'Goodbye, daughter.'

'*No, no, no!*' she sobbed, letting her head sink, her long brown hair falling over her contorted face.

Instinctively Bogdan felt for the little leather bag of his native earth around his neck. It wasn't there. He must have lost it during his flight from the hospital ward. For one moment he panicked. Then he pulled himself together. The loss seemed somehow symbolic of what would happen to him now. He licked his dry, cracked lips and said in German to Colonel York, 'Good-bye, Colonel.'

'Good-bye, General'

'Remember me when you are old — and look after her,' he indicated the sobbing girl.

'I will, General.' York snapped to attention, his hand to his beret in rigid salute, the tears standing in his eyes.

Vera raised her head. 'Alexei!' she screamed wildly. She made as if to dash forward, but Colonel York caught her just in time

Bogdan was already walking to the coach, ignoring the cry, disdaining Sergeant-Major Harte's instinctive offer of assistance, clambering into the carriage unaided, the blood pouring down his arm, his broad back visible for one moment before vanishing inside.

York, supporting the sobbing girl, looked along the train for his face among the hundreds crowding the windows, trying to bridge the insurmountable gap between the doomed inside and the living outside. But it did not appear. General Alexei Bogdan had left them for ever.

The locomotive shuddered. The steel driving wheels raced, trying to get a grip on the gleaming track. They caught. The long line of coaches jerked. The watching women screamed. Children, who had climbed on the low station roof to catch a last glimpse of their fathers and brothers, waved and wailed, sobbing with the uncontrolled passion of the young.

The train began to steam out. Slowly at first, but gathering speed at every instant. The individual faces of the Cossacks staring out at the crowd from beyond the grilles, like convicts from behind prison bars, became a blur and then one last white flash. Then the train was speeding around the bend. A glimpse of the blank back of the mortuary van. Two red glowing lights. Grey steam shot up. Sadly and slowly it cleared to reveal an emptiness. The train had gone.

The gleaming rails sighed and stopped trembling. The signal clicked down with a harsh note of finality. Now there was no sound save the soft weeping of the women.

The great adventure was over. The Black Cossacks had failed. Now they sped to their deaths.

ENVOI

The report appeared on the third page of the Moscow edition of the *Pravda* for 14 August, 1946, just below the figures for tractor production in the Soviet Republic of Georgia for the first half of that year.

It was bald and unadorned. Simply a long list of Russian names, meaning little to most of the Soviet paper's readers. It began with the name of a certain '*Vlassov, A. A.*' and ended with '*Bogdan, A*'.

Thereafter there were a few lines of dull, uninspired text, which told nothing of the years of exile, heartbreak, suffering, pain and torture that the unknown men had undergone.

They read:

'*They were accused of high treason and of being agents of the German espionage service, committing the crimes of espionage, diversion and terrorism against the U.S.S.R, contrary to Articles 58-1, 58-8, 58-9 and 15-11 of the Legal Code of the Union of Soviet Socialist Republics. All the accused confessed themselves guilty. In accordance with the terms of the Ukas of the Supreme Soviet, dated 19.4.1943, the Military Tribunal of the High Court sentenced the accused to death by hanging.*

The report ended with the words:

'*This sentence has been already carried out.*'

A NOTE TO THE READER

Dear Reader,

If you have enjoyed this novel enough to leave a review on **Amazon** and **Goodreads**, then we would be truly grateful.

Sapere Books

Sapere Books is an exciting new publisher of brilliant fiction and popular history.

To find out more about our latest releases and our monthly bargain books visit our website:
saperebooks.com

Printed in Great Britain
by Amazon

56559152R00106